Anyone Who Utters
a Consoling Word Is a Traitor

THE
SEAGULL
LIBRARY OF
GERMAN
LITERATURE

Anyone Who Utters
a Consoling Word Is a Traitor

48 STORIES FOR FRITZ BAUER

ALEXANDER KLUGE

In Collaboration with
THOMAS COMBRINK

TRANSLATED BY ALTA L. PRICE

LONDON NEW YORK CALCUTTA

This publication was supported by a grant from
the Goethe-Institut, India.

Seagull Books, 2022

Originally published as Alexander Kluge, *Wer ein Wort des Trotes
spricht ist ein Verräter*
© Suhrkamp Verlag Berlin, 2013

First published in English by Seagull Books, 2020

ISBN 978 1 8030 9 136 5

British Library Cataloguing-in-Publication Data
A catalogue record for this book is available from the British Library

Typeset by Seagull Books, Calcutta, India
Printed and bound by WordsWorth India, New Delhi, India

Contents

To live a decent day. It's pouring—a relief after the hot days of July. And so I've donned one of my heavier suits and showed up 'dressed'—in full armour—at the office. But the suit is equally fitting for the funeral service of Dr Fritz Bauer, which I'm now on my way to.

The casket is in the cemetery's small chapel, amid some bushy, thick-leaved oil plants. A large floral spray stands up front. The music for the service was single-handedly chosen by philosopher Theodor W. Adorno, sans all supervision. He's arranged for three of Beethoven's late string quartets to be played, in full, paid for by the government: No. 13 Op. 130 in B-flat Major; No. 14 Op. 131 in C-sharp Minor; and No. 15 Op. 132 in A Minor. This is supposedly comforting music. But it isn't. It is ABSOLUTE MUSIC.

Adorno, presumably the only attendee capable of deciphering this music, nods his head with the notes, his hair a mere bit of fleece, in sync with the music's inner movement—in no way according to the lay definition of 'musical', utterly unlike a metronome keeping time.

In his will, the deceased forbade any formal address. The group of mourners is made up of the minor ranks of the government that took shape after 1945 and sought to keep the country on an antifascist course. Since the music performance takes an inordinately long time, and no speeches disrupt the flow, a deep engagement with the deceased arises. The Minister of Cultural Affairs has lost his best friend.[1]

I picture the deceased unlocking every cell in Butzbach prison, addressing the inmates as 'comrades'. The legal administration considered the expression that of a fool. It had tried to limit him, surrounding him with conservative attorneys general who gradually robbed him of all responsibility. But playing the fool was a necessary act of camouflage. Bauer always had files on hand which he used to keep the detectives— holdovers from the old regime in Frankfurt and the Federal Bureau of Criminal Investigation in Wiesbaden—in check. For their every wrongdoing (every relapse into old ways), he'd slip one of their incriminating files into action.

And it isn't clear, incidentally, what he died of in his lonely bathtub. I'd like to follow up on this. After the music ends, the funeral guests rise. They don't quite

---

1 On the other hand, none of the present friends or political authorities would have been available had Fritz Bauer tried to reach out to them before he died, or sought someone to talk to. No one among this country's overburdened leadership had the time or energy required for friendship or human intimacy. 'Anyone who utters a consoling word is a traitor.'—Bazon Brock

know what to do now. There is no one in charge, no one setting the scene. Warden Helga Einsele, who can't stand just standing around, quickly leaves.[2] Undersecretary Eberhard Fricke to Adorno: 'We should talk.' Supreme Court President Curt Staff to me: 'I believe we're both published by Goverts.' 'Indeed.'

Adorno's wife abruptly pulls him away. He's still in the small chapel, basking in the quartet's sounds, and wouldn't mind seeing the concert all over again. But she wants to avoid any potential mix-ups with the deceased and his fate, so she pushes out the graveyard door.

Mrs Ilse Staff has rented out Salon 15 at the Frankfurter Hof Hotel for a reception following the service. Most of the mourners head there. The idea is to reconstruct something of the deceased, especially for his relatives from Sweden, who hardly knew him at all. The Minister of Cultural Affairs uses his hands to imitate some of his hallmark gestures. He recounts an anecdote from Kassel. A five-year-old child wanted to go to school, and wasn't allowed, but just kept running back to class. The headmaster banned the child from the premises, saying it's too early for the child to enrol. In comes the recently deceased, to organize a Q-and-A session. He neither requests the permission

---

2 Either because she was crying and didn't want it to show, or she could no longer endure the speechlessness the deceased had requested.

of nor directly refers to the school system, as he isn't accountable to it. He listens to the child's mother. Turning to the administrators, he asks: Well, why can't the child simply stay, and be left to learn? The Chief Administrator: It's against the rules. The recently deceased: The child shall stay put, and if that happens to be in school, then so be it. The child's mother was incredulous that the problem could be solved so easily. The Chief Administrator replied at once: Yes, but the Minister of Education has decreed that only children of the stipulated age may attend school. The recently deceased: I don't know who will denounce you if you deviate from that decree. But the rules are made by reasonable people, in the interest of reasonable people. In no way does the explicit will of this child go against the interest of this country. Tell that to the headmaster. It never was clear why the child wanted to go to school so badly. Perhaps they had friends there.

In the end, seven men and two women sat around the small table until 5 p.m. Drinks were served. The minister was urgently sought in several parts of the country, but the ministry didn't know where he was hiding—namely, Salon 15. Those present didn't want to part ways with the deceased. As long as they sat there, together, there was some connection to him. When they parted, the fine gent was finally gone. No one from the country's subsequent generations has taken his place.

Rabbits on gravestones, from the film *Abschied von gestern* (*Yesterday Girl*).

Vanished into Thin Air, by Some Strange Coincidence, Like a Gas

The wheels of the mixed freight-and-passenger train headed from Paris to southern Poland rolled onward. Two locomotives pulled the 26 carriages. Propaganda phrases like 'wheels roll for victory' were foreign to the experts overseeing all rail-related traffic throughout the German Reich.

Just outside Flörsheim am Main, a national railway coordinator with discretionary powers stopped the transport. The plan had been for the escort team, consisting of French officials, to accompany the train to Cottbus where it would be transferred to German personnel. The French officials had a poor grasp on the German language. The German railway coordinator instead ordered that the train be unloaded here, on site, and then sent northward, empty. Apparently a crisis on the eastern front made it urgent that provisions (ham from Schleswig-Holstein) take precedence.

The goods (machinery and equipment) and detainees (Jews with French citizenship, arrested in Paris in September, en route to Auschwitz) were forcibly unloaded. The protestations of the French train attendants were duly noted. The two locomotives and carriages drove off.

With the help of the local group leader and teachers serving in the National Socialist public-welfare programme, the 'refugees' were accommodated in an adjacent freight yard and the station restaurant. Those who had been unloaded lay cheek-to-cheek on emergency cots and boards turned into makeshift beds.

Over the following days, many escaped. Some crossed the unguarded French border in small groups. Others were hired as unskilled labourers at nearby wineries that needed help with the harvest and were prepared to issue temporary papers. The wineries' participation was aided by the fact that the French Jews understood just enough German to carry out the necessary tasks.

In the meantime, this transport from France to southern Poland (Auschwitz) had not been 'forgotten'. As long as there are files, administrative processes (and those responsible for their enactment) cannot deny having a detailed memory. All subsequent investigations, however, led only to the equipment and machinery unloaded from the redeployed train, not to the people, who had been registered under a completely different hierarchical division. So a long time passed before it came to anyone's attention at the Reich Security Main Office that the 977 detained Jews had not reached Auschwitz. Furthermore, those responsible were frequently travelling during this phase of the 'extermination project'. In this case, every investigation had a set jurisdiction to overcome—another hurdle to clear.

By the time what had happened at Flörsheim station was finally determined, only 18 of the unloaded detainees were picked up from the station restaurant. Those 18 people who had counted on their luck were killed at Auschwitz. All the rest—that is, the vast majority—'vanished' (seeped out through the countless unrecognized channels, paths and escape routes that lay within the terror system whose confused state, for those few days, lay exposed). Some made it to the suburbs of Lyon. Others went into hiding in northern France (with no papers and no contact with the French authorities, who they avoided for good reason).

First Research, Then Kill

In the autumn of 1941, field researcher Dr Elfriede Fliethmann—of the Race and Folklore Department of the Krakow Institute for German Labour in the East (which had flourished in the two years since Poland's occupation)—was visibly troubled. She shared the same fear as her colleague Dora Maria Kahlich—at the University of Vienna's Anthro-pology Institute—namely, that (speedy as they were with their measurements and questions) they would soon be deprived of their 'research material' by the task force's resettlement and extermination campaigns. Their research was being conducted in and around Tarnów.

Their subjects were large Orthodox families. According to the researchers, these families came from the original proponents of Galician Judaism, with utterly unique characteristics found nowhere else in the world. The researchers' charts compared their findings of this 'racial-anthropological miracle' to the history and development of Galician Jewish emigrants. Department VII ('Enemy Research') of the Reich Security Main Office had recently requested their research documents.

The researchers appealed to their superiors in Lviv, arguing against the ongoing resettlement and extermination measures taking place 'directly next to their research area, undermining their work'. Their complaint explained the situation as follows: The effects that would result from relocation to an inhospitable area and decimation of the population have not yet been researched. Their subjects' physical fitness in extreme conditions, i.e. selection (as shown in Table No. 15, 'Success after emigration to the USA'), could result in qualities that turn an otherwise easily defeated enemy into a much more challenging opponent. In support of this argument, they had distilled world history and presented it on another table (No. 23). Moreover, the 'anthropological miracle' they had discovered was further distinguished by two unique characteristics: one, an obvious homogeneity of descent whose direct lineage could be traced back to Mesopotamia (through blood-composition analysis); two, a richly mixed linguistic heritage. The latter suggests that, over the past thousand years, members of the group in question lived in close contact with vastly different socio-anthropological systems and lifestyles, and therefore are, linguistically and culturally, virtual chameleons; and (if such a group were to be regarded as an enemy) these traits would prove advantageous for the opponent and disadvantageous for the Reich. In this regard, it is only logical that—as was the view of the Division

VII Leader, Brigadier Prof Dr Franz Alfred Six—the anthropologist's approach be: first research, then kill. Ultimately, only researching what is to be killed can yield important insights into the most efficient mode of elimination.

It all happened so fast. The researchers' objections went unheeded. After fulfilling their task, the murder squads moved on. Soon the 'partisan problem' consumed all the occupying power's attention. In any case, the Reich's upper ranks could only ever entertain a merely superficial interest in any of the individual areas of their territory.

A Touch of Liveliness That Surprised Proust

The eight young officers—exactly as they had left company headquarters on the front lines outside Verdun for the weekend, 'disreputable' in their tight uniforms insofar as they stank after the long nighttime journey, but nevertheless ready for amorous adventures—raced into the Duchess of Guermantes' GRAND BALLROOM. Proust noted their arrival. Later on, he sought to get closer to the youngest of these senior officers, whose calling card bore the name Helbronner. Unnoticed by the latter, Proust lingered for some time, making small talk, trying to stay in the vicinity of this tall youth. The writer was intent on capturing the appearance of this war god amid these society folk in a portrayal that would last for all eternity. At the same time, he was also looking to stand out in the officer's memory—the officer who would leave for the front, and perhaps death, the very next day. As Proust frantically jotted down scraps of conversation on the back of a menu, he lost track of the gang of sprightly pleasure seekers who had enlivened the ballroom and then taken off. Proust looked among the dancers, the turmoil of spectators, the lounge area near the toilets and by the exits, but Helbronner was nowhere to be found.

The Most French of All Jews:
Jacques Helbronner

Jacques Helbronner—supporter of Marshal Pétain, friend of Cardinal Gerlier in Lyon, the most French of all Jews, top officer before Verdun, lawyer, member of the Conseil d'État, president of the Israelite Central Consistory of France (excluding foreign and immigrant Jews, who were relegated to a separate organization)—was arrested by the Gestapo in Paris on 28 October 1943. He and his wife were deported on Transport No. 62, from Drancy to Auschwitz, which left French territory on 20 November. Both were gassed immediately upon arrival.

Was he wearing his uniform? He had been when he was arrested. He had also donned all his Orders of the Republic and medals of military bravery. All those decorations had been taken from him at the barracks in Drancy; they were considered provocative, as if they would cause people to rise up against the Vichy regime at the very last moment. The protective coat of his uniform was replaced by plain civilian clothes, as if he were any other man. So did he die clothed or naked? Like all others killed in that fashion, he was unclothed at the time of death. He was no longer the GREAT HEL-BRONNER, who had married into old French money, making his status in France appear set for life.

President Pétain and Cardinal Gerlier were notified immediately after his arrest. He could have been rescued in the 23 days before he was loaded onto the transport train. Even at the border, French officials could have taken him from the train. Over 80 people tried to organize help. Why did the cardinal do nothing? What real risk might the Vichy authorities have run had they attempted a rescue, even if only to cleanse their consciences for the sake of appearances? It's puzzling that nothing happened. Even just sending the Helbronners to Theresienstadt, instead of Auschwitz, would have sufficed. Leo Baeck, Paul Epstein, David Cohen, Abraham Asscher and Zvi Koretz were all deported to either Theresienstadt or Bergen-Belsen, and most of them survived.

Expulsion's Long Roads

A wise man from Salamanca—doctor, theologian, jurist and forebear of Fray Luis de Léon—was a visionary. He could wind his way along the paths of the INTELLIGIBLE WORLD, parallel to the mere world of factual reality, to navigate the tunnels of the future. He never told a soul exactly how he did it. In the period prior to the 1492 edict of expulsion, it became glaring that Saint Dominic's zealous followers posed the threat of persecution.

This sage advised several of Salamanca's Sephardic families to emigrate to Lisbon before the forced expulsion. But they shouldn't trust the Catholic rulers of Portugal for long, either; rather, he advised they continue their journey before 1497, moving on to the more tolerant Ottoman Empire or the Netherlands.

One of these extended families crossed the Atlantic and reached Pernambuco, which was occupied by the Dutch for some time, and then, after the Dutch lost the colony, moved on to Amsterdam. Another extended family settled in the sultanate and spent several centuries there. It wasn't until 1943 in Salonica that some of their descendants fell into the hands of new persecutors, who no longer even bothered basing their extermination plans on religious belief. The Scholar of Salamanca's prophetic gift had endured several hundred years, but by the end of that Platonic Year, after providing a spiritual overview of 26,000 years, it turned out to be a bit blurry.

The Daughter Was Rather Fond of Her Father

The young girl, daughter of a merchant whose family had made it from Spain to Lisbon after 1492, was rather fond of her father. She was touched by the fact that her fingernails, hands, cheekbones and shoulders so clearly resembled his. The family, still stubbornly unbaptized, still wealthy, had been lulled into a false sense of security by their few years in Portugal. Then King Manuel issued an edict that all children under the age of two be separated from their parents (and left to the care of Christian families); the adults were ordered to emigrate. Shortly before these persecutory laws came into effect, the girl's family purchased passage on an Arab captain's sailing ship. The journey was expensive (what they paid in gold and silver nearly equalled the value of the entire ship). The captain, however, was deceitful and had hatched a plot: off the Moroccan coast, a Berber pirate would hijack the ship. The passengers were relegated to the pirate's rule.

The pirate had confiscated all the prisoners' possessions. They had nothing to offer him in exchange for their release. They promised him money if he brought them to Constan-tinople, but he rejected the idea. Untrusting of himself and his own character, he couldn't trust that his passengers would be willing to pay up after being rescued. THERE WAS NO MODEL FOR SUCH A CREDIT-BASED EXCHANGE. The pirate thought it better to dock on the nearest coast and sell his 'goods' as slaves.

The young girl who, as previously stated, loved her father, couldn't imagine him being sold into slavery: he was utterly unfit for any type of labour that might be done by a slave. She feared that, if she weren't able to find a way out, it would mean her family's downfall.

Theirs was a learned household. The girl spoke demotic Greek, still the lingua franca of the Mediterranean. It turned out that the pirate, despite his brutish tendencies and line of work, was an educated man. Each night, the girl sought to attract his attention. They played chess and debated theological matters. Soon she managed to open his mind enough that he saw how far from lucrative—indeed, how worthless—this group of Sephardic Jews would be if sold as slaves. Moreover, she argued, assuming that they would pay up upon arrival at their destination, while clearly not an everyday experience, was a much safer bet than expecting that they'd fetch a good price at auction in any of the nearby ports.

Furthermore, this would mean that the two of them, the girl went on, would have invented a new FORM OF BUSINESS, just as easily as they'd sat there playing chess: it would be an operation as epic as Julius Caesar's when he had freed himself from slavery by offering a series of specific, unexpected and highly unusual explanations. This allusion to the ancient ruler pleased the pirate. He relished the idea of becoming famous for all time like that legendary dictator.

Thus they debated night after night, and were already past Tunis; they now sailed by the coast of Crete. The wise daughter's father later settled up in gold, paying in full for the promises that had granted him and the group freedom. He thereby established a future for loans of this sort, such that, amid the parasitism that always accompanies mass expulsions, forcing people to promise 'money in exchange for life,' a trace of FAITH AND TRUST is preserved.

Starting Small: A File Is Prepared

In May 1937, Dieter Wisliceny, former head of Department II 111 (Freemasons) at the Reich Security Main Office, sat in a makeshift cell in Department II 112 (Judaism). No one would have recognized him yet as the omnipotent decision maker of Salonica, which he became in 1943, or as co-organizer of the Jews' deportation from Hungary in 1944.

Without a typewriter, since he was not entitled to a typist or any such machine, he jotted down the following note to be passed on to the typing pool:

Subject: Position of the Jews in Event-A

Precisely as their wartime service is specially regulated according to §15 of the Military Service Act, in the case of Event-A, the Jews of Germany shall undoubtedly be subject to exceptive law.

Such a law, the wording of which cannot be specified here, must nevertheless be drafted and ratified at the highest level; additionally, it should be formulated to take effect immediately upon the enactment of the Military Service Act.

The security service must therefore take the precaution of establishing a Jewish file in preparation for Event-A, specifically designating Jewish business leaders as well as political and Marxist-minded Jews.

Event-A is the administrative term for a declaration of war. The wording of the note, which was forwarded to central command, with a carbon copy to Department I, was deemed 'awkward' by Dr Werner Best, the department chief. It seems the Jewish file was still a work in progress.

Back before Anything Had Been
Decided for Certain

In 1935, as the administrative authorities were still developing their plan for persecuting the Jews (they sought to secure in-kind advantages and access to foreign exchanges while also limiting the disadvantages of said persecution for the Reich as a whole), the Reich and Prussian Ministry of the Interior delivered a presentation by statistician Dr Friedrich Burgdörfer to the Wehrmacht adjutant's office in the Reich Chancellery, to the attention of Major Hossbach. It contained estimates of the number of able-bodied Jews in the Reich. The presentation was intended for use in drafting compulsory military-service legislation.

The number of Jews and 'half-breeds' within the Reich, the statistician explained, was based on estimates.[3] The book *Die Bevölkerungs und Berufsver-*

---

3 Three Reich Departments (Statistics, Genealogy, and Emigration) as well as the Nazi Party's Racial Policy Office, were responsible for the collection of specific data points. It later became clear that solid knowledge of individuals' descent could only be obtained through local church registers. Without the help of a few thousand pastors, the Reich's central authorities would have had great difficulty identifying Jewish and mixed

hältnisse der Juden im deutschen Reich ('Jewish Populations and Occupations in the German Reich') provides some rough data from Prussia in 1925. Working from the basis that 45 per cent of Prussia's male population was between the ages of 18 and 45, Burgdörfer goes on to summarize his estimates as follows:

Jews and half-breeds of military age: 327,825 (approx. 328,000)

    Summary:

Full Jews who observe the Law of Moses:	475,000
Full Jews who do not observe the Law of Moses:	300,000
1st- and 2nd-degree half-breeds:	750,000
Subtotal:	1,525,000
	approx. 1½ million
Of which are male:	728,500
Of which are male between the ages of 18 & 45:	328,000
From this, subtract approx. 20,000 foreigners	
Total:	308,000

Hossbach went on to note that the number of 308,000 conscripts corresponded to 18 additional divisions—which, distributed over the total armed forces, would be equivalent to two armies. It would appear that the

---

families. Reich headquarters, on its own, had no detailed information on specific places or people.

authorities were considering the establishment of a special Jewish Legion (and, accordingly, warships with Jewish crews). Shortly thereafter, §15 of the (compulsory) Military Service Act excluded Jews and half-breeds from military service.

Forced Sale of a Historic Munitions Factory in Thuringia

The visit from Lieutenant Colonel Dr Martin Zeidelhack, of the Army Weapons Office, at the FLICK/MITTELSTAHL industrial group, represented by Otto Steinbrink, marked the beginning of a broad conspiracy. It regarded the Simson weapons factory in Suhl—whose technical director and managing partner, Arthur Simson, was of Jewish descent—and its sale to Flick. According to Dr Zeidelhack, the sale had been ordered by General Liese and Colonel Leeb of the Army Weapons Office, and was further supported by General von Reichenau in agreement with engineer Keppler, the Reich Chancellery's economic commissioner, who had obtained the approval of the SS Reichsführer. Arthur Simson had already been arrested for treason. While in prison, he had agreed to the general terms of sale, stipulating 'that sale of the century-old company be entrusted to a professional purchaser who guarantees that the labourers and factory production will continue on as is.'[4]

---

4 The company had been founded in 1835, and its plans for 1935 included building an electric steel plant and bar-rolling

In exchange for entering into negotiations, Simson was released. Under the auspices of Reich authorities, a meeting with Flick's CEO took place in Erfurt. He set certain conditions for the acquisition, and was promised that 60 per cent of the army's total demand for light machine guns would be produced in Suhl. As late as 1934, Flick/Mittelstahl had offered Simson 10 million Reichsmarks for the plant. Now a purchase price of 9 million Reichsmarks was agreed upon, but only 3 million was to be paid immediately; 6 million would be paid in instalments over a period of 6 to 10 years. Then even that offer was withdrawn. Simson fled to in Switzerland in 1936. He had no say in the final contract.

Although Dr Zeidelhack had confirmed that Flick/Mittelstahl was ready and willing to take it over, that no longer mattered. Under the leadership of District Director Fritz Sauckel, operating under Hitler's approval, the munitions factory—that dated back to the first industrial revolution and had armed Prussia

---

mill. The factory itself, which predated Simson, had produced weapons for the Crimean War, the American Revolutionary War, the Franco-German War, the First World War, and for Spain during the Rif War. That history, combined with the Reich's impending rearmament, stoked strong expectations. Simson was considered a major expert. For a short while, the Army Weapons Office had sought a way to give him the status of a German, independent of his heritage, by changing his name.

during the Prussian-Danish War—was transformed into the Reich's Wilhelm-Gustloff Foundation. Its de facto value was equivalent to the lifetime of Arthur Simson and his relatives.

A Forced Exchange in Budapest, 1944

The petty-bourgeois magnates from Berlin strode—among an ensemble that included Oswald Pohl, head of Reich Security Main Office Department III, ECONOMY—embarrassed onto the carpets of the salon in a Budapest hotel. The salon had long served as a space for high-level negotiations. In certain places, the characteristics of previous regimes still held sway; such was the case in Hungary, where the Fascist regime was still young but its power already inflationary, hence it must have foreseen the imminent change and its own downfall.

The negotiators from Berlin had just carried out a comprehensive inspection of the WEISS EMPIRE's iron and steel plant. The German Reich's industrial assets depended on the SS taking over the Weiss company to expand its fortunes. The Weiss representative took care not to make a show of his innate negotiating talents, and hesitated to make any offers regarding the post-war period to his opposing negotiators. The aim was to avoid irritation and complete the business exchange as 'smoothly' as possible: the Weiss Empire would be surrendered dirt cheap in exchange for the immediate rescue of the Jewish family that owned it.

All it took was for the Weiss representative to make the most of the opposing negotiators' momentary embarrassment, such that they mistook possession of the plant itself—which would be taken over by a sub-organization of the German Reich—for the rich reward. They were very excited. In peacetime, the assets transferred in the legal paperwork they signed would have been worth a few billion dollars. A small portion of the stipulated price was to be paid into a frozen account in Zurich, and the departure of 52 family members for Switzerland was also guaranteed.

Negotiators Pohl and Eichmann expected the War Merit Cross First Class in gold for this coup. A mere nine months later, the industrial assets they had acquired were in Russian hands. The fleeting nature of such deals was reflected in the grand hotel itself, which hosted the negotiators: since the establishment's founding, each regime change marked a decline in overall guest services. By the autumn of 1944, the Italian staff were no longer dusting behind the figurines that adorned the fireplace. A connoisseur would have noticed the hotel's decadent state. But the officials overseeing the German extermination campaign—upstarts who had never before frequented grand hotels—weren't capable of noticing. Nor, absent all precedents, could these stewards see that Weiss's massive machinery halls, valuable vendors, specialized workshops and even inventions and innovations were of no value in and of themselves—neither to the owners, who were forced to choose between death and selling the company, nor to the acquirers, who were dependent on the German Wehrmacht's incompetent attempts at defending this part of the world.

The Victims Stood on the Rails
of the No. 2 Tram, Waiting

In Budapest, by the corner of the redoubt along the banks of the Danube, the victims were waiting on the rails of line No. 2 of the tram. Those still far from the river were clothed, those already at the Danube's edge were naked. Screams were heard, shots rang out on the shore. That afternoon, the dead lay bloody atop the floating ice sheets. The ice jammed. There were also non-Jews, German soldiers (perhaps deserters) and Hungarian officers among the dead. A member of the Fascist militia, who seemed confused, reported all this to Carlos Branquinho, the Portuguese chargé d'affaires.

Professor Ferenc Orsós, a Hungarian lawyer and member of the International Katyn Commission, said at a dinner party soon thereafter: 'Throw the dead Jews into the Danube, we don't want another Katyn.'

Changing of the Guard:
Doing Away with an Obsolete Plan

A few Hungarian officers escorting 'Jewish labourers' to the copper mines of Bór, Serbia, had attempted in vain to leave some of their wards behind at various railway stations. They had come up with the plan three months earlier—they couldn't overlook the sheer exhaustion of the marching prisoners—but by September 1944 it was already outdated, as the withdrawal was underway. On 6 October, the prisoners reached the hamlet of Crvenka. Ethnic German guards were brought in to replace the Hungarian guards who were sent back. The prisoners were then divided into two groups. About 800 not-too-exhausted men were sent marching onward. The second group of about 1,000 men was taken to a brickyard and murdered by the SS. In Sivac the group of 800, which had just been deemed fit for labour and sent towards the Bór copper mines, was surrounded by an SS cavalry unit. The 'service labourers' were ordered to lie down, and were then indiscriminately shot.

On the Bureaucratic Tracks

The double-track railway line built during the Habsburg Empire's investment boom of 1872, which ended with the bust of Vienna's banks in 1873, still led from Hungary to Poland. There were no other direct connections. The station in Prešov, Czechoslovakia (as was reported by a group of labourers in Slovakia via messengers sent to Switzerland) was the transit point for deportations from Hungary. They came up on the railway from Košice.

The merciless pace of the German-Hungarian campaign against the Jews of Budapest in March 1944 had finally made waves farther afield, especially in the neutral countries. Hungary was occupied by the German Reich, and the national government was removed from office (the prime minister committed suicide). But the occupiers had not gained the upper hand with the administrations of Hungary's railway, postal service, Customs agency, nor parts of the police and army. They were thinking ahead, to the war's foreseeable end, and were not willing to commit crimes. News was leaking through the country's permeable borders, so word of the 'arrests' and weekly death-camp transports reached the World Jewish Congress in Hungary via Switzerland, London and New York. Leon Kubowitzki was head of the WJC's RESCUE DEPARTMENT. Suggestions began flowing in: could Soviet paratroopers or the Polish underground army be on standby to occupy and destroy the Auschwitz death camp on short notice?

Repeated requests had been made (most recently on 31 March 1944, by a Slovak rabbi) to bomb the railway line between Budapest and Poland, thereby making it impossible for the transports to pass. None of the other territories occupied by the Reich had such reliable informants, or any resistance that came so close to becoming an armed insurrection. The easily destroyable 30-metre bridge over a river was a particularly vulnerable point along the railway. It lay directly before a tunnel entrance which such a bombing could readily block. The transports would have had to resort to a long detour via Austria, over strategic railway connections to the Balkans and Greece; in terms of sheer duration, this would be so burdensome that the PARTY OF PRACTICAL THINKERS would have ceased further evacuations. The Union of Orthodox Rabbis in Switzerland shared this message with the Union of Orthodox Rabbis in New York. Isaac Sternbusch passed it along to Roswell McClelland, the representative of the War Refugee Board in Bern. 'We request air raids be carried out on the cities of Kaschau and Preschau.' Reference was made to the Vrba-Wetzler report. In a letter to his fellow associates in the US, Swiss resident Weissmandel added, 'How guilty will you feel if you do not move heaven and earth?'

All these recommendations and instructions were given to John W. Pehle, the US Department of Treasury lawyer, who was also head of the War Refugee Board. He wrote a carefully weighed, indecisive letter to John McCloy, Assistant Secretary of War at the Pentagon.

On 4 July 1944, McCloy responded that, in accordance with Pehle's sober assessment, the proposed airstrikes could NOT BE CARRIED OUT. They would call for considerable air-force support that US troops in the Mediterranean required instead.

At the same time, Rudolf Höss was once again summoned from Berlin to Auschwitz in order to continue preparations for the Hungarian Jews' destruction. He returned to Berlin on 29 July, and was awarded the next higher rank of the War Merit Cross for his additional contributions.

Berlin Childhood around 1937,
with Headquarters in Silesia

Back when the Jewish Mission in the German Reich could still maintain its leased manor in Silesia—the Freie Lehrgut Groß Breesen—young people were sent there for agricultural training before being sent abroad to work the land. Its founding principles mirrored those of the youth movement: 'To journey from being a member of the community—trudging the hard road, confronting oneself—to building true character.' The leader of the Overseas Emigrants' Group was a merchant's son from Breslau nicknamed HANIO, a portmanteau from Hanno Buddenbrook and Tonio Kröger. The members of his HANIOSGROUP had been won over from the followers of another leader, Bert, who was the last leader of the Jewish youth group Schwarzes Fähnlein ('Black Battalion') and later fought in the French Resistance.

HANIO, whose real name was Hermann Ollendorf (born in 1917), was adored by a Berlin merchant's son nicknamed TÖPE, also known among fellow group members as TÖPER (a superlative of TÖPE). HANIO had made a mistake on a canteen bill he owed, and came up several hundred marks short. People believed him when he said the unexplained charges were merely a matter of sloppiness, not a hidden intention to enrich himself. But the mishap left a scar. At the same time, HANIO had begun to doubt whether he could join the group trip because he didn't feel physically fit enough (he had kidney trouble) to settle abroad. So he booked a hotel in Breslau and overdosed on sleeping powder. We merchants' sons, his follower TÖPE (born 1920 in Berlin) later explained, aren't physically suited for the work of founding of new countries or cultivating fields reclaimed from the desert or jungle. But we are young and strong-willed. TÖPE had lost his best friend (after HANIO), Herbert Stern (born 1919 in Nuremberg), nicknamed STELLA, just the prior summer. He had drowned in Groß Breesen while out for a swim.

I'm no Hans Hansen, TÖPE continued in his report, but HANIO loved me and I loved him. All of us, overwhelmed as we were, set all our energies in motion. And so the year after HANIO's death I went to the Netherlands, and I now teach at the university in Berkeley; my friend Jochen Feingold, who back in Groß Breesen had been the best at irrigation and cultivation, went to Kenya, where he became a farmer and, later, political advisor. We've stayed in touch and remain (despite the bitter losses all around us) believers in the Jewish youth movement.

Spartacus' Belated Victory

Alexander Pechersky was the son of a Spartacist. He was not a political commissary, but he was a Jew. The German defence officer examined the passport of this prisoner of war without realizing the danger this man posed. He saw only his physical and mental fitness for labour. And so in 1943, Pechersky, Lieutenant of the Red Army, was transferred along with 25 fellow Soviet officers to the Sobibor extermination camp. With his arrival, a local plot to rise up and escape gained traction. By then the inmates were convinced that the economic benefits their labour offered the Reich would not spare them from death, and that their strengths would be sucked out and ultimately liquidated by the machinery of extermination. One can repent for crimes, but one's race cannot be stripped away.

The administrative arrogance of the camp's SS overseers had prevented them from infiltrating the prisoners' ranks with moles. They couldn't send their own men, because such hard labour would have destroyed them. Nor could they have explained why, after expending all their strength, such spies wouldn't then be sent off on transports alongside all the others to their death. Nor could they recruit traitors from among the prisoners, as was the practice in antiquity. Nazi official Franz Six had previously pointed out that ancient Greek rulers convinced slaves to work for them, betraying their fellow slaves, by promising subsequent release; the camp administration forbade any such promise and, because that historic practice was widely known among the prisoners, such a proposal would've been implausible anyway.

Thus the network of conspirators preparing the uprising went unnoticed by the camp administration. 'Yet only [. . .] when a young Jewish Red Army lieutenant, Alexander Pechersky [. . .] joined the planning group, were concrete steps rapidly taken.'[5]

Using a pretext, the SS guards were lured into the workshops on the day of the uprising. They were then attacked and killed. About 80 armed prisoners stormed the main gate. The machine gun posted at the entrance didn't fire. At this point, the uprising led by Pechersky and his engineer colleague turned into a mass escape. Upon arriving in the woods, it turned out their plans for what was to happen afterwards, once they were free, hadn't been made entirely clear. The network of conspirators had assumed there would still

---

5 Saul Friedländer, *Nazi Germany and the Jews, 1939–1945: The Years of Extermination* (New York: HarperCollins, 2007), p. 559.

be contact between the leaders and their followers, so that the general location and precise spot where the groups should go could be decided after re-evaluation of the circumstances as they developed.

Pechersky and his confidants also expected that any surviving SS-camp overseers would've been killed in the meantime, so that no news could reach the authorities in the surrounding area. They counted on having such a head start on their persecutors that, even if any caught up, one of the armed camp inmates obeying their orders could lure them into a trap and liquidate them. After three days, they aimed to be so deep into the woods that their recapture would be impossible. But the mass flight had destroyed the communication structure required for such plans.

The German bloodhounds—all Reich police-academy alumni were trained in how to set up dragnets—barricaded all the streets, paths, railway stations and bridges within a wide radius. Then motorized commandos started the search. Most of the escapees were captured.

Pechersky's sqaudron had already gone eastward and disappeared far into the woods by then. He alone, son of a Spartacist, was able to keep his six group leaders in constant motion. They moved steadily towards the River Bug. The exhausted escapees repeatedly quarrelled while marching onward. Occasionally, they even proposed turning back to hunt more prey. Each evening Pechersky held a meeting, and again won approval for all for his proposals despite being in the minority: 'Stick with the majority, even if they're wrong.' He considered it essential that any errant ideas within his followers be eliminated: especially among those who just wanted to take a break or pursue further prey, thereby leaving behind clues for their enemy to track them down. After several weeks, the long line of refugees, now far past the banks of the Bug, ran into a group of partisans. Danger still loomed on the horizon. The political commissary advising the partisans demanded evidence that the escapees weren't agents of the Third Reich. It took a while for them to reach a decision, because everything had to be cleared with their higher-ups. Meanwhile, a fast friendship had already grown between the partisans and Pechersky's group—they'd carried out campaigns together, so aggressive confrontations would no longer have been possible.

The Impotence of Conventional Agreements in the Face of Kaltenbrunner's Men

Puccini's TOSCA was performed, as it was every year, at Rome's Teatro dell'Opera in the autumn season of 1943. In the third act, dawn breaks over Rome. Cavaradossi, the tenor sentenced to death, bids farewell to his life. The music's notes represent a fresh breeze blowing into the ancient city, much as the lively chorus voices the living cells of the delinquent man's body—the high hopes of a man imagining he still has another chance to sail away, fleeing the tyrannical country with his lover. Shortly thereafter, he stands before the firing squad and is shot to death. The police chief of Rome, Scarpia, had previously promised Tosca he would spare her lover. He does not keep his word. So the viewer feels Tosca is in the right when she kills Scarpia. Numerous German officers and their Fascist comrades, not to mention Rome's arguably apolitical ruling class, had this series of scenes firmly in mind that year, whether they had seen the opera or not.

The chief of the German security service in Rome, SS-Obersturmbannführer Herbert Kappler, did not draw his ideas or conclusions from the performing-arts world. He was a practical man. From his office, he had a broad view out over the city. He had too few police at his disposal. He was preoccupied by the threat posed by the arrested Carabinieri, as well as how he might best control a general population using disarmed yet still dangerous Carabinieri patrols. Himmler issued an order that he use the German occupation of Rome to send the city's Jews northward. At that point, such deportations lay as far from Kappler's mind as the idea of mass shootings. He wanted to use the existing transport trains to send a portion of the arrested Carabinieri forces to northern Italy. He summoned the two most important leaders of the Jewish community, Ugo Foà and Dante Almansi. He demanded that Jewish entrenching battalions be established to defend the city of Rome, as well as the delivery of a PENALTY PAYMENT, 50 kilos in gold, within 36 hours. Providing all that, Rome's Jewish population was to remain untouched.

Moreover, it seemed to him that the persecution of Rome's Jews would be further complicated by a serious structural injustice: the wealthy Jews lived in the city centre and could be hard to capture, while the poor Jews remained in the ghetto, near the Vatican. At the time, the chief of security operated amid a calm sea of consensus on all sides. The Vatican offered the Jewish community a papal loan to cover the 50 kilos in gold. Kappler received universal recognition for the 'elegant solution', the details of which remained unspecified. On 7 October, the collected gold was loaded into the sealed compartment of an express train and sent to the Reich Main Security Office. LATER IT BECAME CLEAR KAPPLER COULD NOT KEEP HIS WORD.

Embassy councillor Eitel Friedrich Möllhausen supported Kappler's line with telegrams to the Foreign Office in Berlin. General Rainer Stahel, Wehrmacht commander in Rome, also toed their line. But then a group of 25 SS officers arrived directly from the Reich: Theodor Dannecker's unit. Its subordinate ranks were relatively minor. They came with instructions from the Reich Security Main Office. On 16 October, they arrested 1,259 Roman Jews. The roundup triggered 288 phone calls and telegrams intercepted by the British. Most related to mitigations or objections. For example, mixed-race people and individuals in mixed marriages were separated from the rest of the group. Afterwards, 1,007 Jews remained, including 200 children under the age of 10. They were locked up in the military academy under guarded watch. From there they were sent to the Tiburtina rail station. From there they were sent to Auschwitz.

The morning of the raid, Countess Enza Pignatelli alerted the Vatican. She prevailed over the telephone operators and managed to reach Cardinal Luigi Maglione, Vatican Secretary of State. For a moment (because of her high social rank) she even had the Pope's ear. Maglione summoned Ernst von Weizsäcker, the German ambassador. Maglione told him that, if the raid continued, the Pope would mount a protest. Weizsäcker replied that such a move could trigger a reaction on the HIGHEST LEVEL from Germany. Are you implying that the Pope would be arrested and the Vatican would be occupied by German troops? the church leader asked. Are you even allowed to report on this conversation? von Weizsäcker asked back.

Up to this point, the British interceptors, who were reconstructing those discussions using the phone calls and telegrams immediately after they left the Vatican, were able to follow along. But they didn't know how Maglione responded to von Weizsäcker's last suggestion. Purportedly, the former had agreed with the latter on keeping the conversation 'friendly', and left all subsequent action up to the experienced German diplomat's discretion.

In an attempt to strike a balance with Kappler's original line and 'save what was to be saved', 90 senior officers, diplomats and influential individuals were enlisted on the Italian and German sides. They were unable to do anything about Dannecker's pack of 25 DETERMINED SS officers, who had already requisitioned the trains; the deportees were already rolling northward on the railway through central Italy.

During a 2012 conference at Columbia University, the question was raised of precisely how the well-laid plans of such a close-knit, corporately protected network of plenipotentiaries—further supported by a tightly woven safety net of long-established logic, and additionally strengthened by deep consideration—could (from a moral standpoint, as would become clear AFTER THE WAR) ever have been so readily thwarted by a such a small team of men shipped in for the occasion (not even brothers in faith, but men merely following orders). The conference was a joint venture between the departments of Business Management and Contemporary History. A series of subsequent questions were posed: How, under present-day conditions, would one respond to the persistent pressures of a small minority when it invokes connection to a broader central command? How can the majority of communicators, who want to take the opposite course of action—action which, however, is commanded not by any headquarters but, rather, by tradition and inertia—reinforce and mend their torn network? Human WILLPOWER, which appears strong, doesn't strike me as actually being strong, Anselm Haverkamp rebutted. It's a relic. Is it comparable to the expression 'will to power'? one of the Americans from a group of business economists asked. Not at all, Haverkamp replied. The necessary nucleus, acting only temporarily and tearing through the aforementioned network (something that could only be pulled off by one or two of the 25 men), draws its energy from the chain of command spanning from the Reich to Rome. Such a chain of command consists, linguistically speaking, of threats. Is it possible to counteract such threats with counter-threats? someone asked back. The group of 25, like ambassadors from an alien world, invariably act like barbarians, as a concentrated charge, someone from the crowd answered. Any one of their opponents could swiftly isolate them. Herein lies the threat: anyone who draws his weapon against such an opponent and sends them packing would, an hour later, himself be isolated.

The conference had already dragged on for hours. Parti-cipants broadened the topic to include examples from our time, in search of concrete instances of such RUTHLESS WILL tearing through the web of *our present-day* civilization. Haverkamp offered the case of a fourteenth-century Dominican who, along with seven companions, invaded an imperial city and established a terrorist regime that lasted an entire year, despite the fact that the local city council, leading guilds, townspeople and the entire nobility directly opposed his tyranny. Haverkamp then compared that to the stubbornness of German Grand Admiral Alfred von Tirpitz, who in 1912 used his fleets to extort the emperor, chancellor and the entire Reichstag into building more battleships: a small group dominated the larger whole. The organizational theorists weren't of the same opinion, and asserted that Haverkamp's thesis was merely psychological. No, he replied, it is literary. It provides commentary on the examples. Could it perhaps have been the one-sidedness, the sheer primitive simplicity of their objective, that made that group of 25 men seem so powerful in Rome? As daylight waned, a sense of conviviality spread through the conference. The majority found the question excruciating. They'd have been glad to see the events that took place in Rome in October 1943 swept away like a shift in the wind. Hans Thomalla, a visiting composer from Baden-Württemberg, suggested writing an opera with the working title 'Tosca 2'. It would be a series of short scenes about the deaths of policemen and security forces, or henchmen and hangmen—deaths that would occur before the consequences of their evil deeds had unfolded. The majority of conference attendees came to the conclusion that the only way to fight the fanaticism inherent in any chain of command based upon the threat of isolation is to destroy it before it arises.

A Certain Kind of Rigid Willpower:
Unstoppably Destructive

Richard Haldane, the British Secretary of State for War, visited Berlin on behalf of his cabinet in February 1912. He had organized negotiations with the Kaiser and Chancellor to directly address a twofold, interconnected issue: In the case of conflict between Germany and France, would England remain neutral? The British position, which lay in clear opposition to this German request, was: In exchange for said declaration of neutrality, would Germany immediately renounce all further reinforcement of its naval fleet? And just how political and binding would such an agreement prove?

Had such an agreement come about, it would probably have guaranteed peace throughout Europe for at least 30 years. Neither France nor Germany had any reason, as long as they weren't threatened, to wage war against each other. The same held true for all other European participants in the negotiations.

Lord Haldane's goodwill and openness to reaching a consensus could have led to a settlement, but were instead precisely what led to catastrophe after the negotiations had failed. The cause of this failure was the dogged determination of Admiral Tirpitz, leader of the German Imperial Navy, whose plan—based on his so-called Risk Theory (build enough German dreadnoughts to force England to avoid confrontation)—was already obsolete. His calculations were still based on the idea that by 1923, the combat strength of German battleships would be on par with those of the Royal Navy. He spoke of keeping them on 'equal footing', although a fleet's strength is measured not by footing but by firepower. It also later turned out that the German navy, blockaded into the coastal regions of the North Sea, could at no time have posed any significant challenge to the British fleet. But, based on the widespread popularity of the naval associations Tirpitz had organized throughout the Reich, he was able to essentially extort the Kaiser and Chancellor. Meanwhile, Lord Haldane had dared to bear the brunt of the British tabloids which had previously been hostile to Germany. The crucial blow, however—according to British historian John Röhl—was dealt by a CERTAIN KIND OF RIGID WILL-POWER, which set Admiral Tirpitz apart from the Kaiser and Chancellor, whose 'softer' and more civilized (or less united) characters were no match for his. Thus Germany's friend, Lord Haldane, swiftly turned into an opponent. The soon-to-be-former friends would have no more chances to pull the emergency break and avoid a collision with the sheer weight of fate. In 1914, war broke out.

The Sheep of Rome

A man considered himself, his family and his ancestors (many of whom were ministers) important. He had climbed the ranks to become Secretary of State of the German Reich's Foreign Office, but had then been forced from his position—not least because he no longer believed the empire could achieve victory—in much the same way as his representative, Colonel-General Franz Halder, had had to leave his post in the Army High Command. This man went to Rome as German ambassador to the Vatican. Under the eternal auspices of this enclave, he hoped to once again conduct the kind of political dialogue he had participated in so actively before the war.

His new path was not as clear as he had foreseen. Trip wires quickly appeared, including the so-called Jewish question. Immediately after German troops occupied Rome, the Jewish ghetto had been evacuated, and the inmates shipped out on rail transports. This was a disturbing picture. How was one to discuss with other diplomats—conversationally, animatedly and politely—power balances following the war's foreseeable end if broaching such a topic could immediately trigger the question of whether or not it was true that the people who had been evacuated from Rome would soon be killed in Poland?

Only a few weeks later, this ambassador of the German Reich was seen as the 'Sheep of Rome'. Local, effectively incapacitated officials dressed as SS officers had torn up his plans. He had previously spoken of his aim to have a 'calming' effect, but now, in the eyes of the world, he had the opposite. Did he really believe his own words? How, asked the Sheep of Rome, could the people asking such questions—in the Vatican, in Roman society, in the diplomatic corps—be so sure that the deportees had been sent off to die? What had taken place was initially kept secret, even from him, the ambassador of the German Reich.

From then on, no one at any of the lavish Italian restaurants where he hosted dinners for Rome's most respected elites believed in the 'discursive powers' of this eminent representative of the Reich. He was later sentenced to imprisonment at the Nuremberg Trials, but not for his failure to honour the promises he had made in favour of a 'peaceful' solution for Rome's Jewish population. He had lost his rank as negotiator of the hoped-for final peace accord.

Witnesses from Another World

I am the Commander of Radio Surveillance with the British forces in the Western Mediterranean. I am responsible for intercepting communications throughout Rome and the railway lines leading northward. We hear everything the talkative enemy says through telephone, telegram and radio lines.

We work much like angels or gods. The amphitheatres of ancient Rome pale in comparison to the panorama that spreads out before us from our listening posts. My strict vow of secrecy forbids me from naming the ways and means by which we obtain our (almost complete) information. Outside my military role, I am a mathematician and Assyriologist at Oxford University. Six hundred surveillance teams report to me, including those stationed on Royal Navy ships. All day and all night, the Italian peninsula is criss-crossed by planes carrying our radio spies at high altitude.

I once read in a sci-fi novel that extraterrestrials are listening in on us humans, but their professional ethics forbid them from intervening (to avoid betraying themselves but, above all, to avoid cross-contamination). Similarly, we must preserve the intelligence we gather in safe storage while not interfering down on the ground—in Rome, for example—as it might betray our otherwise impeccable surveillance.

Thus we never warn suspects of their impending arrest, nor do we give any clues to our parachute forces standing by, or to agents in the Italian capital working for our cause. I consider our role—charting and collecting intelligence while staying above the fray, which sometimes also prevents us from saving human lives—comparable to that of Ashur, the deity 'who withdrew from humankind'. This was in the later phase of the northern Mesopotamian city, before the 'time of great silence'.

Collusion Suspected upon Homecoming

During compulsory labour we were surrounded by our German vanquishers and guarded by the SS, one of the seven forced labourers reported. When panic broke out during a nighttime bombardment, a working-class comrade from Champagne—the only non-Russian man in our group—was shot by an SS aide-de-camp. We took his wallet and watch so we'd have something to remember him by.

At the end of April, we found ourselves in the zone of Austria occupied by Americans. We were trucked to Linz, where we waited for representatives from our Russian leadership. No one came, so we took over a steamboat—the Saturnus, which was intact but unmanned, moored on the banks of the Danube—and decided to take it to the Black Sea and on towards home. We got about 200 kilometres downriver, and were nearing the town of Melk, where the Soviet-occupied zone began, when our ship was stopped. We were taken to a camp, interrogated and searched to determine whether we had collaborated with the enemy. The mere hint of suspicion was shameful. We had no evidence to defend us from indictment. Based on my age, I was conscripted.

Overwhelming Emotion as a Form of Defence

The interviewer, whom a Viennese foundation had sent to the East, had been given a list of addresses. That, he reports, is how he found a woman in western Ukraine—formerly Galicia—who as a 15-year-old girl had been forced to do heavy labour for the German Reich. She was now an old woman. At the time, the interviewer said, he had little experience interviewing people who were hesitant to recall bitter experiences. Even his first few questions, he noted, quickly led to her silence.

We arrived at the woman's house around noon, in the sweltering heat, he continued. She seemed to suffer a serious illness. We had to refuse the fish dishes she offered. There was no river for miles, so where the fish was from, and how long it had lain in the heat, remained unclear. Nor did we feel like accepting the shots of vodka. Without the customary exchange of hospitable gestures, the conversation couldn't get off the ground. The old woman called over the daughter of a former colleague to help out. She and the woman's mother had been forced labourers in the same unit. The daughter came and took on the role of hostess.

But this didn't set the right tone for the conversation either. The woman broke down crying the moment I asked anything. I tried changing the subject, and asked her about two photographs pinned to the wall, of a boy and a handsome man. The boy was this woman's son, who had died at the age of 14. The other picture was of her husband, 'who was hanged in front of his lover's window last year'. The woman began to cry again. Meanwhile, the daughter who had been summoned to help, jotted something on a personal-ad page from an Austrian mail-order marriage company. She asked us to take the clipping with us and post it in Austria. First and foremost, she wanted to get out of here.

Being forced to do hard labour from 1943 to 1945 and then, upon returning home, having to endure accusations of 'cooperating with the Germans' had been deeply hurtful experiences. That, along with her financial situation and utter lack of hope regarding her own fate, got in the way of her telling us the story of her past. Now 72, the woman had reached her twilight years, and could scarcely afford to entertain comforting fantasies of the future. The woman strove, the interviewer noted, to recall a few bland memories. But she in no way wanted to relive the most degrading episodes. At the same time, she must have had a talent for improvisation and initiative. On one of her medical reports, a doctor had apparently written that she was allowed four sick days.˙ Almost as an aside, she remarked that she had written a one in front of the four, so that she was allowed to stay in the sick ward for an additional 10 days. No one questioned it. Had her forgery been discovered, she could have been sentenced to death. But the woman wouldn't think back to the past for more than a minute. Overwhelmed by the situation, we politely bade her farewell, said the last line of the interviewer's report.

Overloaded by Sheer Mass

In the summer of 1942, the number of forced labourers from the Eastern territories in the German Reich reached its peak. The units carrying out raids and organizing the transports were already overwhelmed. By the beginning of 1943, companies had begun rejecting many of the labourers being sent to the Reich because underage, incapacitated and sick people were being included, so they were loaded right back onto return transports to the occupied territories of the Soviet Union. The condition of those shipped back home (often to the wrong place) appalled the local population—this was yet another organizational error that made itself felt anew every time another load of people was picked up. These errors were brought up at the Central Conference of Reich Labour Commandos, and it was proposed they be prevented by better staff training going forward. In the meantime, the VALUE OF THE LABOUR FORCE, which the Reich had easy access to in the previous year but was now increasingly difficult to obtain, was recognized in principle by Reich leaders. They gave university seminars on the topic. The main takeaway: if a large colony or other foreign territory, such as India, were to be overseen by organizers trained by National Socialists, the mistakes of 1943 would prove to be a valuable experience, since the most lasting lessons can only be learnt by trial and error.

Calling It a Day by 17.00

Around 17.00 the killing stopped. The witnesses and guests invited to the execution had left the grounds of Fort IX an hour before. Even the 12 snipers responsible for the post-execution rounds—shooting those who were NOT YET DEAD in the neck—were tired, and the fact that they were not being poured any more schnapps was supposed to encourage them to carry on. The 800 guards and 100 Latvian service personnel marched in columns back into the city's various quarters.

Away from the fort, at the second execution site—but far from the mass graves—several groups of evacuees from the capital were waiting to be led deeper into the forest. The fact that they hadn't yet grasped their fate and showed no signs of worry proved how well it had all been organized, and strict order was maintained even after work. Had anyone run away, or if the guards suspected the victims had fully understood the situation, they would have been rushed to the execution site. And so, once the executioners had knocked off for the night, the evacuees stood in the field virtually unguarded, unheeded by Fort IX's central leadership which was now headed into the city to celebrate.

Reports of what happened to them over the following days differ. According to some, they were shot dead on 8 December with the remaining evacuees from the Riga ghetto. But where had they spent the nights? According to other reports, parts of the group were transferred to Kovno, while others remained in the forest, where they were administratively 'forgotten'; a few of them eventually found the local partisans' hideout. The partisan group itself was so small that it fell 'below the radar' and was no longer detected; the recordkeeping was full of holes. They were the living dead, as if they had been shot alongside all the others that 30 November. They were left behind after everyone else had called it a day.

The Peculiar Purview of Architects

Here I see the list of commissioners who went to Riga at the request of SS General Jeckeln. The 8th and 9th SS commissioners are listed as architectural experts, historian Arno Hilpert says, somewhat surprised. They dealt not with buildings, he continues, but with the proper removal of corpses. Indeed, his French colleague replies, you have to consider the term in its broadest sense: ORGANIZATION IS A SPATIAL ISSUE. It's a question of storage. Ensuring that its planning is adequately aesthetic and practical is the domain of architects. Determining the right place for the executions, how the dead can most efficiently be transported to a different place, where they can then be stored underground—all that can be considered a single structure, like a building. It can be designed barbarically, or according to the standards of public buildings from the classical period. The SS's Architectural Division not only built barracks and sanctuaries but also arranged for the construction of execution sites. They were also responsible for designing the surrounding camps, whose construction wasn't under the jurisdiction of the SS camp administration but of the Organization Todt—the Nazi corps of engineers. Similarly, petrol stations as well as pipelines and coal

transportation can also be considered the purview of
architectural design.

An Intellectual-Property Violation

Chief Engineer Prüfer at Topf & Söhne, who arranged corpse storage at Auschwitz II, filed a patent for one of his inventions: the 'Bonecrusher', more precisely described as a 'bone-breaking-and-shredding machine'. Physically and chemically speaking, neither the bones nor the highly aqueous soft tissue of human and animal bodies can actually be 'burnt'. Bones survive the flames, and only the fatty parts of meat burn—the rest is charred into coal. Cremation invariably leaves behind too many traces capable of pointing to the vast number of dead. Hence, as the Germans retreated from the East in 1944, their 'terror troops' endeavoured to more thoroughly expunge all traces of their crimes: initially, the bodies had been buried in shallow graves; the perpetrators now sought to put them deeper underground, and also tested out new chemical solvents with the aim of dissolving them into nothing, making them vanish into thin air.

However, because of Prüfer's patent and the fact that a few prototypes of his machine were still available, the required chemicals could not be obtained. The Bonecrusher did just that with the excavated remains, down to the molecular level, rendering the evidence unrecognizable: a destructive principle tailor made for the modern age. But because TIME WAS OF THE ESSENCE, no one respected Prüfer's owner-ship of the underlying intellectual property. It was as if copy-right were no longer enforceable! Furthermore, the use of subpar knock-offs of the machine discredited his original invention. The Bonecrusher wasn't even used in slaughterhouses after the war, as Prüfer had expected. As patent-holder, he had aimed in vain to grow old and rich from the fruits of his idea.

Where Empathy Manifests

Erich von dem Bach-Zelewski, Obergruppenführer of the Waffen-SS, had won the winter battles of 1941–42. Through-out the following marshal mud season, he personally oversaw the execution of Jews and partisans, and then promptly suffered a breakdown. His haemorrhoids—known among comrades as 'Trooper's Joy'—flared up and proved tough to treat.

I can only comment on this as a doctor. I draw upon my practical experience in military hospitals, as well as my experience reading our national poet Gotthold Ephraim Lessing and the British authors who influenced him. From this perspective, I must insist that it is precisely in professional soldiers of firm character—so-called REGULAR SOLDIERS—that, if suppressed for long periods, the indispensable human trait of 'empathy' most violently erupts. And it physically manifests in the places most subject to the exercise of willpower: the anal sphincter, or other parts of the nether regions— where some patients succumb to sensitivities that make their skin itch and burn.

On Saturday at about eleven o'clock in the morning, the Reichsführer's aide-de-camp, Karl Wolff, drove over in the staff car (doctors and nurses had gone to the capital for an event, so emergency service was arranged). Bach-Zelewski had undergone a minor intervention in the morning, and not yet fully recovered from anaesthesia. He lay in bed trembling, looking 'frail' and hunched over and displaying all the characteristics of a 'coward'. Wolff hurried up the stairs so quickly that I had no time to alert my chief physician, Dr Graditz, who was in his staff quarters at the time. Wolff was appalled by his comrade's condition. He tried to hold the patient's hand, in hopes of comforting him, but then let go and rushed off, visibly perturbed. The staff car sped off, and I followed.

That afternoon, the phone rang. This time we were prepared. Dr Graditz took the Reichsführer's calls. Over a series of long-distance calls that lasted until evening, he sought to counter the devastating impression that one of the Reich's most valuable SS leaders had received incompetent medical treatment. But it was ultimately the sight of his inwardly torn, uncontrolled nature that had struck comrade Wolff as 'appalling'. This man here—our patient—was a human being, not a general.

Bach-Zelewski was hallucinating. He was unable to ward off 'recurring memories' of his actions in the East. I would have called in a knowledgeable healer of minds whom I had met during my studies in Vienna in

1928, who might have been able to help. But, to my knowledge, he had since escaped to Argentina via Trieste. A list of the entire military hospital medical and nursing staff, complete with their appointment details and career history, was requested by the Reichsführer's office; it appeared that a kind of 'revenge campaign for their mistreated comrade' was being mounted.

The Pain of a Perpetrator: The POST-TRAUMATIC STRESS DISORDER of an SS-Obergruppenführer[6] following Eastern Deployment

The impression Bach-Zelewski made upon Karl Wolff, who had driven out on Saturday to visit and look after his comrade, and who in turn told the Reichsführer-SS of said impression, led to a chain of telephone calls and inquiries directed to Dr Graditz, the Reich-SS doctor responsible for his medical treatment.

A typist was immediately summoned from a Sunday off to write a letter to the Reichsführer, worded as follows:

Re: SS-Obergruppenführer Bach-Zelewski

To the Reichsführer-SS, H. Himmler, Berlin
Reichsführer!

---

6 *Obergruppenführer* was one of the highest positions in the Waffen-SS hierarchy, corresponding to the Army rank of Commander General. The painful haemorrhoidal inflammation paid the patient's high rank no heed. The tortured psyche invariably seeks physical expression.

71

To confirm and supplement yesterday's long-distance call, I hereby submit an interim report on SS-Ober-gruppenführer Bach-Zelewski:

As previously reported, once the intervention's immediate aftereffects subsided, the healing process began—but over the last eight days the resumption of regular intestinal activity has caused some difficulties. The reason for this was that, following the operation . . . opium was used as an intestinal sedative, provoking the usual thickening of the fecal column. Repeatedly during the last few days, the intestine had to be cleared by hand, a procedure carried out under brief anaesthesia in order to protect the patient's highly affected nerves . . . A return to regular, unassisted bowel movements can be expected in the next few days. The very slow healing process . . . is regrettably common after haemorrhoid surgery, since the mucous membrane of the anal sphincter cannot be fully immobilized during the procedure . . . At the same time, the extreme degree of general as well as nervous exhaustion in which the patient came to treatment following his service in the Eastern territories has become noticeable. Since adequately treating the patient's mental state is not easy—he suffers in particular from recurring memories of mass shootings of Jews that he himself directed!—I am largely devoting myself to his treatment. I strive daily to re-establish his mental equilibrium, as well as attend to the personal wellbeing of Mrs Bach-Zelewski, who I am permitting, upon her request, to spend her nights in the hospital . . .

I sincerely regret, Herr Reichsführer, that the impression SS-Obergruppenführer Wolff got during his visit on Saturday—which was completely distorted by the effects of anaesthesia— led to the logical yet mistaken presumption that SS-Obergruppen-führer Bach-Zelewski received inadequate and incorrect medical treatment and nursing care . . . My hope is that in approximately two to three more weeks he will be fully healed and in stable enough condition to undertake a several-week recovery at a sanatorium without necessitating further medical treatment.

A mere half year later, Bach-Zelewski resumed his duties as SS- and Police Chief of Central Russia, and, in October 1942, assumed the post of plenipotentiary overseeing the combat of criminal gangs. That Saturday, according to the report filed by Karl Wolff, he was trembling and 'looked like a wreck'.

A Generous Disposition

Morally speaking, he was no better prepared than his peers in Italy's diplomatic consular service. But he did believe the desire motivating his German colleagues, to 'exterminate the Jews of Europe', was a passing fad. In the conversational style that betrayed his background and status—Piedmontese, a northern Italian dialect infused with dry wit—he described Hitler as 'an actor' whenever he publicly proclaimed his hatred of the Jews. The diplomat deemed the display of such strong desire—especially destructive desire—fake; it struck him as 'far too extravagant for any man, unsuitable even in the dining room, bedroom and boardroom'. In 1918, Hitler had attended a public-speaking school that had recommended precisely that type of tirade. It worked, and became the recipe for his success, as well as the tool by which he saved himself whenever he got into trouble. Or so the diplomat had been told. But his seemingly light banter contrasted with his earnestness as a practitioner. He knew never to underestimate the ready violence of an SS search commando. He hadn't dared travel into German territory for a long time now, not even with his diplomatic passport. He wasn't by any means audacious, but he was able to 'talk the talk' so well that he appeared reckless, even though in the professional realm he relied exclusively on direct observation and extreme caution.

Serving as Italian Consul General in Nice for the Italian-occupied area of France, Alberto Calisse had banned all distinctive markings on passports held by Jews. It had earned him a degree of opposition from the Vichy regime, which exerted pressure on him, since the French were also responsible for the passport system in the Italian zone. He reacted with dilatory tactics, neither denying nor admitting a thing. Meanwhile, some non-French Jews with valid, unmarked passports had managed to escape to Spain and Portugal by sea. Then a delegation from the German central command came in to round up Jews from his territory and transport them to Poland. At the trial, they grew rowdy. He himself was by no means a Jew-lover, yet he also saw no reason for enmity. His opponents tried to allege that he was involved in a conspiracy. In their aim to suppress Jews, they drilled him, and asked whether he had taken bribes. The Ministry of Foreign Affairs in Rome gave him cover.

Calisse was on good terms with the local military commander, a general from the Bersaglieri corps. Deploying his Piedmontese gift of gab during negotiations, rather than his earnestness, gave him an advantage. Chatting with him was enjoyable. Both these qualities had strengthened his spirit of resistance against the persistent Germans, who, seen from the Italian side, were impolite strivers incomprehensibly keen on annihilation. Calisse told them they weren't to draw their pistols on Italian territory, 'neither at us, nor at Jews'. They weren't even allowed to kill a rival here, his general added. The behaviour of their 'allies' struck the two friends as 'unrealistic'. They took them for mistaken men, not murderers. This categorization diminished the sense of terror emanating from the envoys. In terms of personality, it seemed clear from their jovial exchanges that these supposed German messengers of death were merely putting on airs. Surely they weren't capable of acting on the rage they so readily displayed.

By then, both decent lunch breaks and siestas had become unthinkable. Calisse brought a large group of Jews he believed were no longer safe from the hotels they were staying in along the Riviera (Vichy gendarmes were already guarding these hotels) to recreation centres in the French Maritime Alps, designated as rest quarters for Italian officers. He had the Jews stay here, where they didn't have to sign in with their home address. A plan was prepared for their departure. Consul General Calisse was later shot dead in a small town on Lake Como—facing out over the water, and labelled a Fascist alongside 28 others—by insurgents. That same day, not far off, a man who had escaped two years prior thanks to Calisse's generosity was driving around in a jeep. He had since become a member of the US Army, and managed to discover his former rescuer's whereabouts (following his transfer from Lisbon to the US, he had joined the US intelligence service). Unable to locate Calisse, he saved other Fascists from death. It was unjust. Yet it occurred to him that Calisse's core message was to be GENEROUS, rather than getting hung up on one violation of justice or other. He therefore saved another group of Italian Fascists from being shot, and drove them by truck to one of the communal prisons, where judicial procedure dragged on until no more death sentences were being issued.

Just Barely Escaped

Without any directive or order, a reserve captain in charge of guarding US prisoners of war had gone against the advice of his Waffen-SS Scharführer. The latter was his subordinate, a squad leader who carried out the daily selection of prisoners loaded onto trains and sent to do hard labour in the caves of the Harz Mountains. He had gone through the prisoners' barracks and separated out everyone he regarded as Semitic. He determined this by looking at their facial features, and also drew conclusions from individual prisoners' names and how they responded to his questioning. Thus a group of young GIs, mostly from New York, were separated from the rest, queued up and sent off down a country road under the watch of four guards and the aforementioned Scharführer. They were to be sent southeast, and would therefore be absent upon the expected arrival of advancing American troops.

In the late afternoon, an exchange of fire could be heard west of the camp. The captain had promised to follow the column of selected POWs and then provide further instructions on how they were to be dealt with.

But that evening the captain died during a volley of submachine gunfire. The prisoners marched on, down streets and through villages, without any rations. The guards felt chained—against their will—to their wretched captives. They would have gladly moved on alone, each man for himself, in order to more quickly get back to home turf.

When they received no additional marching orders in writing, the Scharführer knew it was a red flag. If stopped by a patrol, they would not be able to prove that they were moving through the country at their captain's behest. Suggestions on how to proceed were brought to him, both by the prisoner's spokesman and his own guards. In one case, the Scharführer rejected the suggestion made by one of the guards, a secondary-school teacher: shoot the prisoners. Worn down and hungry, the group crossed into an area where the local population had begun to rebel. Continuous rain and low-hanging clouds made orientation difficult. So, as they left a small town, the German guards were glad to spot American jeeps approaching. The Scharführer formally handed over his command to a US officer, and the Jewish POWs' spokesman stood by his side. Who are these prisoners of war?, the officer asked. He could see for himself that they were Americans, but wanted to know where they were coming from. Were there any lists? They are American Jews, answered the Scharführer, now visibly afraid.

They fed the liberated GIs, then put the Scharführer and guards on the bonnets of two cars and drove them to the nearest headquarters for interrogation. Ultimately, he brought these men to safety, said one of the two US Intelligence Service interrogation specialists, pointing to the Scharführer. He led them on a death march, replied the other, We've caught him attempting murder. Then you would have to shoot him, said the first. But neither wanted such a responsibility. Convening a US war tribunal seemed impossible, given the time and their location. It was also unclear to what extent such a court martial could issue a verdict on German prisoners of war for their activities before capture. Then let's not even take them as prisoners of war, I don't see them as enemies, they're just German criminals, insisted the second. The first, somewhat more level-headed officer dismissed the idea. That night, the Scharführer and guards were transferred to a camp near Erfurt. Here, nobody knew anything about the fallen captain's crazy selection criteria or the death march. Thanks to a chain of coincidences, the Jews from New York and their guards (one hesitates to call them lucky) barely escaped with their lives.

The Unexpected Homecoming of a 'Full Jewess'

Gerti had never seen her father so excited. She had come home. Her mother—who had thought her marriage to Gerti's father, the chief engineer of a large industrial plant, and a gentile, would protect her—had been arrested.

It was now 1944, and new guidelines had been issued. Marriage to a gentile was no longer a protection. Where had her mother been taken? Could she be rescued? Gerti and her father tried to mobilize everyone they had any relation to—that is, everyone who was still in town. The mayor (whom her father had called upon) knew or said nothing. Their connections in the criminal-investigation department had no leads. The police department probably hadn't been responsible for her arrest. Gerti, too, came up against a wall of silence. Someone recommended she contact the parish pastor. He must have heard something. But he was bound by his vow of silence. Gerti grew outraged: Where had her mother been taken—which direction did they go? He blessed her, a daughter in distress. But why wouldn't he speak to her? She put a map of Germany in front of him. His official position might have prevented him from *saying* anything, but nothing could stop him from *showing* her where her mother was. He pointed to a location near Jena.

Gerti got moving. She took the train from Dortmund, switching lines seven times. Finally, once in Jena, she took the tram to the end of the line and headed down a country road on foot, in the direction of the spot the pastor had pointed to on the map, where there was supposedly a forced-labour camp supplying Jenoptik.

A car loaded with milk containers approached. Gerti flagged it down. She was wearing a long, flowery dress, and was an attractive young woman. The drivers let her in. Where to? The labour camp, she replied. She thought someone close to her was there, and wanted to visit. Sure, the drivers answered, that was where they were delivering the milk, too. Could she come? Yes, if she promised to drive out with them again the next morning. No problem!

In the camp's barracks, Gerti learnt that a woman matching her mother's description was staying in one of the single rooms. She had asked the inmates of the large dormitory, sociable women, who gladly showed her in. The woman turned out to be Gerti's mother. She came to meet her in the hallway. Everyone else had agreed to give her the single because she looked like a lady. She joked about it. The social norms of the outside world—of the time before—applied even here, as long as the camp administration didn't get in the way. Mother and daughter warmly greeted each other. Gerti was given a cot next to her mother's. Contact had been established. Now, after she returned to Dortmund, she'd be able to mobilize her network and try to get her mother out.

As promised, the next morning Gerti joined the helpful lorry drivers as they headed for Leipzig. As she got out, the rear tyre of the vehicle, an old banger whose machinery wasn't very responsive, ran over her knee. Luckily it had been unloaded, so was relatively light. Her knee was bleeding, but didn't seem broken. She didn't want to bother the friendly drivers, so she hid the injury. She bound her knee with her undershirt, and used her last bit of strength to get to Leipzig's central station. At the railway-station rescue centre, she had it bandaged and was given an injection. She had no ID, and was taken for a refugee from the bombardments that had recently shaken the city.

On the express train to Berlin, the only remaining seats were in First Class. The compartments were full of soldiers. Gerti was scared, but so exhausted that she resolved: No matter what these men might do to me, I have no choice but to sit between them. The seat was narrow. Nobody laid a finger on her over the next few hours. In Berlin, she knew a student with a place she could stay.

Upon her return, her father notified all possible connections to try and free his wife from the labour camp. The authorities saw through his plan, and believed they knew how to make him see things their way. Her father became viewed as a troublemaker. He was told to divorce. Shortly thereafter, he lost his position as chief engineer of the plant: no longer considered 'indispensable wartime staff', he was drafted into the Wehrmacht reserves as a Pioneer Officer. Meanwhile, Gerti's mother had learnt that the Jews in the labour camp were to be transferred to Theresienstadt. It was winter. The organization between the defence industry and concentration camps had already grown porous. Gerti's mother was able to walk out of the camp alongside a fellow inmate and reach Erfurt on foot. Without any identity papers, she stayed in the cellar of one of her husband's relatives until the end of April, and then slipped back home to Dortmund, where she found her daughter alive. That May, Gerti's father came home from the Western Front.

Administered Atrocity

On 28 October 1941, military commander Lieutenant General Karl-Ulrich Neumann-Neurode was informed by telephone that, at dawn, Lieutenant Colonel Karl Hotz, Field Commander of Nantes, had been shot dead by unknown assailants. Nothing in his private life or his professional life provided the Secret Field Police investigating the case any clear motive for the assassination. Neither they nor the French criminal investigation department found a culprit. The simplest solution would have been for the French investigators to provide one. Frenchman Henri Adam was considered, since he had been at large in the city at the time of the crime, and was then arrested for his involvement in an explosives attack on a soldiers' recreation centre. Without any evidence, however, French officials refused to provide a sacrificial lamb. The Secret Field Police was trained to be objective—per the tradition established by Baron vom Stein—and did not wish to encourage them in that direction. Neither rigorous identification checks at roadblocks nor house searches helped yield any result. Thus, the *crime with no perpetrator* was considered an act committed against the

German Reich as a whole and, under martial law, called for hostage executions. There were rumours that the murder had been perpetrated by British paratroopers.[7]

It was this (unconfirmed) tip that caught Hitler's attention. The situation's urgency was reflected by how swiftly the news reached headquarters and was answered: despite the difference between Nantes (still dark out) and Berlin (already daylight), the message sent at dawn received a reply early that same morning. Following a quick conversation, the chief of the Oberkommandos der Wehrmacht (OKW, Wehrmacht Supreme Command) in Paris asked that orders for RETALIATORY MEASURES be drawn up within just one and a half hours' time. The Führer was of the opinion that the French should be punished in such a way that they 'pleadingly beg England to refrain from further attacks in France'. The chief of the OKW indicated that 100 to 150 hostages would be shot, while offering a reward of 1 million Francs in gold for information leading to the perpetrator's arrest. He hadn't come up with the proposal—it was hastily arrived at by a quick

---

7 British prisoners of war could not be shot as hostages because, under martial law, prisoners of war cannot be taken hostage. Who, exactly, could be considered a hostage had to first be defined by a legal act (i.e. by military government decree): for instance, French nationals held in custody at German-run prisons.

vote among staff officers from the Departments of Defence, Justice and the French administration. The French military commander then said he intended to shoot 100 hostages from different ranks, arrest more hostages, offer 1 million Francs in gold at the expense of the Vichy regime, and extend the citywide curfew in Nantes. The call from Berlin arrived at 10.30. The military commander's reply was transmitted to Berlin at 11.50. At 13.30 General Wagner announced that the Führer had approved these latest measures.[8]

General Hilpert, leader of Army Group D in southern France, added to that a proposal that the hostages' execution be postponed, so that the offered reward would have time to produce an effect. The firing squad would only carry out the execution if the announced reward didn't lead to the perpetrators' capture within three days. The Führer's decision (once again, not issued by Hitler himself, but by his staff) was that 50 hostages were to be shot to death immediately, and the rest within 48 hours of the perpetrators' capture. Meanwhile, posters went up listing a reward for clues leading to the perpetrators' whereabouts: 15 million Francs in cash, equivalent to 1 million gold Francs (not payable in bills).

---

8 The sheer speed of all this excluded any chance that Hitler himself expressed any opinion; an answer from the regime's apparatus was sufficient.

The incentive to earn 15 million francs was a machination. Such a promise made it impossible for any of the authorities to infiltrate the dedicated circles of any resistance movement. Even now, it seemed far more promising to prevent the executions by producing a single offender. The reward was high enough to persuade French detectives to 'produce' such an offender. The various sides busily telephoned one another, and this was considered the 'most elegant' solution by all. The individuals to be executed were selected from different hostage lists. The authorities on the German and French sides wanted to avoid a perceived 'vote'. Instead, they went with the order that resulted (partly by chance) from said lists: communist members of the National Assembly, trade union secretaries, agitators, 'partisans' and prisoners arrested for illegal possession of firearms or for having assaulted German soldiers.

As it turned out, two of the prisoners were still at large when Karl Hotz was murdered. They were removed from the list. Minister Pucheu told the German Ambassador that the French side would be distressed if three members of the Executive Committee of the Nantes Frontline Soldiers' Federation were executed. They had been arrested on suspicion of having helped the federation's secretary plan the escape of French prisoners of war. They had been acquitted but not yet released, due to the prison administration's inertia. As a result, these hostages were added to the list of those who were to be shot during the second round of executions.

Thanks to a poet 'loaned out' to the German Defence Department's Commander-in-Chief in France, we have detailed reports on the practice of hostage shootings and reprisals. Part Latin jurisprudence (on the French side) and part barbarian law (as in the Sachsenspiegel medieval law code), the two came together somewhere in the narrow corridor between mass murder and martial law. The principle of reprisals was defined as early as the Franco-Prussian War of 1870–71, and codified in the Land Warfare Convention of 1907. It is the product of an 'administrative ratio'. When the will of the people gets entangled with that of the authorities, who (on all sides) are also entrusted with the right to instigate war, said authorities also determine the actions taken to neutralize all resistance in an occupied country. Such instruments are abstract in nature. Thus the memory of the First World War–era 'blood pump of Verdun' was expected to transform an indefinite number of French citizens' willpower into a newfound desire to capitulate. The most striking way to exert pressure, which is also the most transparent in its abstractness, is to take hostages and issue punishment for 'crimes with no perpetrators' through merciless massacre. Assuming—wrote the poet (whose subsequent report noted the exact composition of hostage groups to be shot, including groups that could hardly have been suspected as perpetrators, especially hundreds of Jews)—that we'll be driven to the other side, and would then (as an enemy of the English) have a chance at upsetting the balance between Germany and France, we should be glad if these measures led to more hostage shootings. The mutual outrage between our occupying forces and the general population would result in an irreparable split.

In that regard, said Captain Jünger, we should not proceed down this path of escalation any further than absolutely necessary. On the other hand, said his friend Carl Schmitt, in Spain's war against the Netherlands a remarkably harsh reprisal (considered impossibly harsh)—the murder of Count Egmont, a Knight of the Golden Fleece and cousin of the King of Spain—fortified the Duke of Alba's rule for 10 more years. That was so effective he didn't need to carry out any more reprisals. So, in the case of Spain, things were dead quiet. But, the poet replied, that created a rift between the southern Spanish provinces and the Netherlands. Alba *lost* Holland. He never *had* it, replied Schmitt. As if we three could decide such a thing, Wildermuth, the poet's superior, concluded the conversation. Good thing, he added, that we have two thoughtful men in positions of leadership reflecting on such things in the here and now, independent of any apparatus, determining the course of action: like chess players, but without the game of chess.

For Administrative Reasons:
No Exceptions

The head of the Reich Security Main Office wrote to ask Martin Luther, head of the German Division within the Foreign Office, to reject an offer from the Spanish government that 2,000 Spanish Jews sent to a French concentration camp subsequently be interned in Morocco. According to the letter, the Spaniards would be unable to effectively guard the Jews in Morocco. Furthermore, such an arrangement would also render the measures planned for after the war—either to evacuate them to the east, or use them as a bargaining chip in the interests of the German Reich—unfeasible.

In his reply to the Spanish Foreign Ministry, Martin Luther provided an additional argument: releasing individual Jews, or even permitting their internment on foreign territory, would set a precedent. Luther had indeed obtained a telex from Rudolf Schleier, adviser for Jewish issues at the German Embassy in Paris, but it contained no such additional justification—merely his approval of the planned negative response.

As if in Another World, Separated from All the Rest by an Invisible Wall

On 23 July 1944, the 1,750 Jews of Rhodes, together with the 96 Jews of Kos who had been arrested and sent to Rhodes by boat, were transported on barges headed for the mainland. Due to inclement weather, the vessels soon sought shelter in a bay, and didn't move into the open sea until 28 July. The Turkish coast was in sight, and they were within flying distance of the British airfields in Cyprus, so the area was fully under British Naval control. The barges moved slowly. On 1 August, they arrived in mainland Greece, where the evacuees were loaded into freight cars.

The transfer was inspected by a Spanish consul who had been alerted by his Italian colleague in Athens. The diplomat believed he could do no more than make an appearance and show his opposition to the guards, essentially sending a message: 'The world is watching what is happening here.' None of that prevented the deportees' loading and departure. The transport trains were sent out onto the rough, often single-track Greek railways and given priority over all other traffic. On 16 August, they arrived at Auschwitz. The prisoners were taken directly to the gas chambers. In all, 151 deportees from Rhodes and 12 from Kos survived. Due to contagious diseases, they had been separated from the others and left behind at various train stations along the way.

The Iaşi Pogrom

On 26 June 1941, in the capital of the former Principality of Moldavia—which, in retrospect, should never have been freed from the tolerant Ottomans— 'retaliatory strikes' instigated by Romanian and German intelligence officers against the Jewish population began. After the mass murder, the wagons of two transport trains sitting in the freight yard were filled with Jews. The doors were then sealed with lead, and the trains sent off to no destination in particular. The first train (later found standing on the open tracks, abandoned by the conductor and staff) held the bodies of 1,194 people who had died of suffocation and thirst.

'Desinteressement'

A word that circulated in the Third Reich's administrative jargon and was considered a 'lofty expression' (used in the ministry council and upwards), originally used on the occasion of Finland and the Baltic States' sacrifice in the wake of the 1939 non-aggression pact with Russia, read: DESINTERESSEMENT. In and of themselves, foreign words were not considered valuable according to the philology of the Third Reich. This expression, however, trickled down from the upper echelons of the diplomatic corps into the vocabulary of many educated National Socialists. It indicated a bold and determined version of non-interest, a kind of disinterest: a distinction that divides the world—into a realm of interest to the Axis and all the rest.

Regimentation

Germany's League of Jewish Women, founded in 1904, had grown into an umbrella organization of 50,000 members across 450 clubs by 1935. Renowned doctor Hertha Nathorff held a lecture on feminine hygiene for one of these clubs on 18 November 1937. She had to submit a manuscript of her lecture to the Gestapo beforehand for examination; she, an expert accustomed to speaking freely, was instructed to read the lecture from the manuscript. She did so in the presence of a Gestapo official, sent to monitor the event and ensure its punctual conclusion by 22.00—whereupon the doors were promptly shut, no questions allowed.

How Hitler Shines before His Comrades Thanks to His Tactical Approach to the Jewish Question

On 29 April 1937, the day before Walpurgisnacht, Adolf Hitler gave a speech to the national comrades at the National Socialist Ordensburg Vogelsang, an elite military school:

> My party comrades! . . .
>
> The Führer state—our Nazi state—has no fear of genius, that is what differentiates it from democracy. If, for example, one of our district leaders were in a democracy, then he would have to constantly worry that some talented underling might take his place. He'd be thinking, 'If the guy carries on like this, in no time at all he'll have the people's backing, and then he'll pull ahead of me. Bam! So much for all my hard work.' . . . So, in a democracy, you have to make sure no new talent comes to the fore . . . That's the self-preservation principle there. (*Laughter.*) That's not the case in the Nazi state, because you know for sure that you can still be talented,

but you cannot get rid of the other guy . . . There is, therefore, basically no such thing as making a demand in the party, it doesn't exist. What would that even mean, for the party to make a 'demand'? I read in a newspaper a few days ago—I'll have to have the man come in so I can talk to him a bit about this problem—he wrote: 'We demand that Jewish shops now be marked as such, and that Jewish businesses be registered.' In the *newspaper*: 'We demand!' Now, I have to point out, you see: From whom, exactly, is he demanding this? Who can arrange this? I alone, that's who. And so Mister Editor here is demanding, on behalf of his readers, that I do this. First of all, long before this here Mister Editor had even heard about the Jewish question, I had already thoroughly dealt with it; *(laughs)* Secondly, this issue of registering has been considered over the past two or three years, and will eventually be carried out either way. Because the end goal of our entire policy is clear to all of us. It's all about not taking a single step I might later have to take back, and not taking a single step that harms us. You know, I always push things to the very limit, but I don't go beyond. You just have to have a sense for it, you have to be able to sniff it out: 'What else can I do, and what can I not do?'

(*The crowd cheers.*) This also applies when fighting an opponent. (*More cheering and loud applause.*) I don't want to demand that my opponent fight, I don't say 'Let's fight!' merely because I want to fight, instead I say: 'I will destroy you! And now, may my wits be with me, I'll corner you so you can't even strike me, and I'll land a blow right to your core.' That's it! (*Shouts of 'bravo' and applause.*)'

The literary scholar Joseph Vogl compared the structure of this speech (how it matched the reaction of his comrades, and the relief the speaker displayed at every applause) with the speech given at the Hofbräuhaus on 8 November 1942, in which he discussed Stalingrad. Again, he made the case of his own side's mobility, maintaining their tactical advantage without losing sight of their goal. Even the rhetorical flourish of the MODEST ASSERTION appeared in both: Hitler said German troops had long since conquered Stalingrad, it was now just a matter of quelling a few minor, isolated Russians, and he wanted to avoid another Verdun. Vogl sketched out the speeches of 1937 and 1942 as if they were musical scores. The cadences and crescendos turned out to match, rising and falling in tandem. They offered up an internal view of Hitler's mind as, surrounded by comrades, he recovered for a moment from the challenges posed by reality.

The Jewish Threat

40,000 Jews with nothing left to lose, Minister Goebbels urged the negotiators in the Reich Chancellery to imagine, are at large in Berlin. After the evacuation of thousands of Jewish citizens to the Baltics, an organizational failure prompting vigorous protest from numerous embassies and a massive wave of criticism from within Germany, further arrests and deportations were postponed. Now they were to resume.

I have no desire, Goebbels exclaimed, to let some 22-year-old Eastern European Jew put a bullet in my belly. He was referring to the discovery of the Herbert Baum Group, communists primarily of Jewish descent who had committed acts of sabotage. Furthermore, they were armed. It would be dangerous, the Propaganda Minister added, to send these Jews to Siberia (a territory Germany hadn't even occupied in February 1942), because local conditions there might allow them to regain a vitality that, as an ethnic group, they do not currently possess.

A Day Trip to Vilnius, 2 September 1941

'You can almost see the exact spot where Russia begins,' Propaganda Minister Joseph Goebbels, ever prone to exaggeration, remarked as he gazed out at the landscape through the aeroplane's porthole. He was implying that, somewhere on the vast snow-covered plain, there was some visible difference between marsh and steppe, some way to distinguish between the fields and huts he considered Poland and therefore part of the Reich. After a stopover in Vilnius, we flew onward, in the direction of Smolensk. Typical November weather. Into a blizzard. The airfield in Smolensk reported: zero visibility. So the minister's aeroplane returned to Vilnius.

That night, the minister phoned Berlin (from a basic hotel, the 'first place in town') to deliver a 'sharp and precise denial' of Roosevelt's assertions. The US President had said in a speech that day—Liberty Fleet Day—that Germany was dividing South America into four zones under a German protectorate and abolishing all world religions.

Goebbels wrote in his diary: 'Late at night we took a short walk through snowy Vilnius. A dreary Central German town. I would not want to be buried here.'

On the Occasion of a Remark by Joseph Goebbels, 'Bourgeois Man Must Be Eradicated'

A close friend of Ernst Jünger in the Army Personnel Office, an 'ironclad man' trained as a shock trooper for the Battle of the Somme, was of the opinion that there are only two types of man suited for the officers' corps or enlisted ranks: the peasant, and the bourgeois. Certainly, he added, while seated with Jünger in Paris and debating these elemental types, there is also the SOLDIER. This third type, he claimed, is essentially a fusion of the first two. If such a SOLDIER is relieved of his duties or otherwise expelled from his circle of comrades or the situation at the front, then his character will split back into its two basic elements, and always favour the dominant one, thus essentially reverting to one of the two. Perseverance (characteristic of the peasant) and daring (characteristic of the urban bourgeois) again emerge, separately. Without the gaze of his comrades, Jünger confirmed, the prized fusion—upon which the army's command structure and the principle of 'orderly warfare' (the ability to act without the guidance of another) are based—breaks down.

A Miscarriage of Justice

In April 1945, a single southern German detention centre housed a group of convicted traitors from several regional jurisdictions. The arrival of US advance units was expected the following day. But then the decision makers responsible for the convicts' cases dispersed. Everyone had fled. In the entire facility, not a single trained executioner remained. The crew now consisted of just two jailers, one gatekeeper and one junior barrister (transferred here after suffering a severe injury during armed military service). They spent the night in a state of confusion, constantly awaiting either an experienced executioner to carry out their charges' death penalties, or an overriding order that would free them from the existing order to execute their charges.

Around four o'clock in the morning they set to it, knowing that once their enemy arrived it would be too late to carry out the executions lest they be culpable of high treason. But killing convicts in their cells was also a grave offence against the Fatherland (albeit not quite comparable to crimes such as murder, theft or homosexuality, all punishable by death in the civilian courts). Once they had started, they realized how difficult such executions were. They had no guidance, nor any personal experience of how to deliver a deadly blow to a prisoner sentenced to life. Scuffles broke out, since the prisoners, at their captors' mercy in their solitary cells, still screamed and fought back. The gatekeeper was the strongest of the four, and even working in tandem they had difficulty getting to each delinquent's neck in order to strangle him. Nor did any of the four know precisely when death could definitively be pronounced (and what signs to look for). But they were determined (and had all agreed) that they didn't want to leave behind any witnesses to their crime. The sheer awkwardness of their actions led them to conclude they were reprehensible. Therefore, not a single sign of life could linger in those they had 'executed'.

They were in a hurry. They wanted to leave the scene before dawn. Five of the traitors killed them. The US patrol, which forced the prison's gate open later that morning, found the dead—each cell a testimony to the fray that had taken place—and called in US ambulances to send the bodies to the nearest higher-command post.

A Jewish Lioness's Battle for Her Baby

On a grassy common in Vilnius where Napoleon's troops once bivouacked, next to a large hospital complex, Lithuanian accomplices had erected a barbed-wire fence. The Jews arrested and detained here had trampled the original grass. The overcrowded gathering spot was now a large mud pit.

According to one report, a young lady of about 22, wearing an expensive gown and mink stole, held the shoulders of her four-year-old son with one arm while throwing herself to the ground in front of one of the Wehrmacht guards, her knees in a puddle, and kissed the man's boots. She begged for her boy's life. The nervous German, who sought eye contact with one of his comrades to no avail, pushed the tip of his shoe against the young woman's lower jaw (in an attempt to keep his balance). She then clung to his knees all the more, adding the other arm which had been holding her son. The soldier's comrade, a lance corporal, finally met the sentry's gaze and came to his aid. He grabbed the four-year-old and threw him over the fence. The woman immediately ran—her shoulders still bearing all the attributes of a lady, although she was clearly no longer considered one—to a spot along the fence where she could reach across, grab her son and move towards one of the hospital entrances.

That's precisely what he intended, the lance corporal later explained. He wanted to free his comrade from 'distress', from the grip of that 'wild woman'. He thought he had seen something like that in the circus— how to throw a piece of meat to distract a lioness from her attack victim—when a lion-tamer had been in a similar predicament. There were enough prisoners gathered in this particularly tight space. Surely they could do without two of them. It would have created an undesirable scene, the lance corporal added, had a German soldier fallen into the mud with a 'lady' clutching his knees.

In the office of the local doctor, the young woman was able to straighten up a bit. Instead of her fur, which one of the nurses kept, she was given a simple shawl. She then took off through an exit opposite the fenced-off area and, leading her child by the hand, got to the railway station and boarded a train (her muddy, battered, bleeding knee hidden below her skirt). Its route brought her out of immediate danger, far from the area of active persecution, and it was widely reported that she was then, thanks to a Luftwaffe officer in Smolensk, taken in as a seamstress and walk-on by the baggage train of a theatre on the German front. The entertainment troupe headed south and reached Odessa, in the

Romanian occupied zone. As later emerged from her report, the enterprising woman (still essentially a girl in a grown woman's costume) had sewn a hefty sum in foreign currency into her expensive dress. Thus she managed to escape through a Romanian port and head to Turkey. From Constantinople she continued on to Cairo, Lisbon and ultimately London. The entire time she held her son, who had meanwhile turned six and a half, firmly by the hand.

A Counter-Intelligence Officer's Report from Odessa

Six weeks after crossing the Russian border, we were assailed by doubt. An eerie foreboding crept through the staff officers. The invigorating feeling we'd had during the Greek campaign, that we'd reap rich spoils, had vanished. We ultimately had NO NEW COAST TO STORM (although the Black Sea spread out before us, it was not the boundary of our planned advance). We had the distinct impression that we were no match for this limitless country. This was the morale with which we occupied Odessa, in order to then leave it to our Romanian allies.

Curiously, our enemy had not destroyed the docks. Did that mean they planned to return soon? Nothing unnerved us as much the massive fleet of vehicles parked there; upon closer inspection, we noticed that all the equipment had been rendered unusable. According to reports from our informants, Red Army soldiers and sailors had gone underground and spread out through the city. Over 200 kilometres of catacombs lie just below the city surface, with 160 known entrances. In hindsight, we now understood why the

Russian soldiers had disappeared into the sewers before our very eyes, and didn't react when we threw grenades at them; they had long since run off through the caverns and tunnels. Almost every mansion has access to these catacombs through its cellar.

I myself manage the liaison office between the German intelligence service and the local Romanian service. I report to my superiors, whose offices are in the Romanian General Staff in Bucharest, as well as to the 11th Army. On Tuesday, 21 October, the building of the Romanian Central Command in Engels Street (the former NKVD building) was evacuated following receipt of a tip which later turned out to be mere rumour. For several hours, the staff officers couldn't tend to their work. As a result, when two men claiming to be Communists called on 22 October to say they were going to blow up the building, their warning was disregarded. At 17.50, the headquarters actually did blow up. It was clearly a remote-controlled explosion, apparently carried out from the catacombs. Two German lieutenant commanders and a coastal artillery captain were dead. German corporals and personnel totalled an additional 46 corpses. They were then lined up in front of the building's ruins. The Romanian division lost 110 men. A few minutes after the disaster, two large headlights from Romanian anti-aircraft artillery shed light on the rescue getting under way in the dusk. According to troop reports, on the morning of 23 October, on a vast square bordered by a wooden fence near the docks, thousands of Jews were shot to death. The square was the size of a fairground. Six German and four Romanian platoons lined up and got to work. One 'pass', including removal of the bodies piled up in mounds, took about 12 minutes.

Massacre as Reprisal for an Assassination in Odessa

The staff officers of the 11th Army's counter-intelligence service based in Odessa included Sonderführer ('special leader') Hermann Stransky. He reported to his superior, expert intelligence officer Erich Rodler, in Bucharest:

> The mounds of victims' bodies piled up on the aforementioned execution site could not readily be removed afterward. They had been doused with petrol and set ablaze, but only partially burnt. Furthermore, pouring still more fuel onto the fire did not successfully expunge the distinct signs of mass execution. Yet their removal seemed opportune in light of the expected reopening of the port facilities and docklands (where even uniformed personnel were only allowed entry if they had a special pass) for much-needed supply by sea. Although our intelligence staff boasts many experts, including archaeologists, none of them were practiced in 'moving mountains'. There weren't even any Pioneer units nearby. What had we done? We couldn't sleep.

We could not shoot into the mountains of corpses using anti-tank guns. That would have merely crushed the proteins into smaller bits. The attempted burning had only worsened things. Originally, the corpses still could have been removed by auxiliary troops, loaded onto horse-drawn carts and transported elsewhere. This was no longer possible once the proteins and other substances had been 'glued together' by the heat of the fire, and thus rendered inseparable. They could no longer easily be split into smaller portions. Ultimately, we divided the problem in half: on the eastern part of the square, we cleared a track leading from the mountains' outer edge into the middle, for the auxiliary troops to haul wagons. From there, they could detach smaller pieces and remove them. The rest was covered by a series of large, interconnected tarpaulins (an idea offered up by naval officers who had used the same approach to cover their ships in the tropics). Thus, we hoped, the irredeemable scars this episode had left on our minds and memory would, in time— at least as a reality in the outside world—dissolve. But, long before such a process could run its course, Odessa was recaptured by the Russians (and I was sent back to Berlin). The Red Army's advance troops must have got an odd impression of our occupation as they retook the city. We have no way of knowing whether they even attempted to interpret this 'testament to our deeds' and rapidly forge further westward. Contrary to our expectations, the Soviet propaganda machine did not seize upon this evidence or wield it to its own ends.

Spaniards without a Fatherland

Only after the death of Spanish physician Ángel Pulido Fernández from Madrid was it discovered that he had saved more than 500 Sephardic Jews living in Salonica. Practicality so completely determined his actions that he had no way of knowing their consequences. In 1924, as an influential Spanish Senator, he had arranged for King Alfonso XIII to issue a decree that the descendants of Spanish Jews expelled from Portugal in 1492—now living in south-eastern European and Mediterranean territories—could obtain Spanish citizenship in Spain's embassies and consulates. The offer remained valid until 1930. Of Salonica's Jewish population, which numbered slightly over half a million, 560 people claimed their Spanish passports. This saved them and their descendants in 1943. They had already been arrested and detained in a transit camp near Salonica's central station when the Spanish consulate in Athens, alerted by Greek attorneys, intervened and attested to their official status as Spanish nationals.

[*A journey around the globe*] The Spanish passport holders were separated from the other deportees and evacuated in wagons under the close watch of diplomats working their way down the list of names. Unlike the other transports, these prisoners were not sent to Poland and the death camps; instead, they were sent to a concentration camp in the German Reich. From there, they were sent clear across France to Spain, processed through a transit camp (accompanied by German representatives who worked their way up the same lists as before, now in reverse order), and sent on to Casablanca. Soon after the Axis powers had withdrawn from North Africa, they reached Palestine, and the majority then went on to settle back in Thessaloniki.

[*An incredible encounter*] During a trip down the Danube in 1880 on a vessel run by the Imperial and Royal Danube Steamboat Shipping Company, a group of business travellers heard Doctor Fernández speaking Spanish and proceeded to address him in an antiquated dialect. It turned out to be a fifteenth-century Spanish that Sephardic emigrants had brought with them. In the four centuries since, it had evolved separately from peninsular Spanish. The people speaking this curious dialect were Spain's 'lost children' who had faithfully preserved the country's linguistic roots. By the time Doctor Fernández met them, the Kingdom of Spain was rapidly nearing its demise. Cuba, the last of its colonies, had been taken from the empire by the

United States of America. The Basque Country and Catalonia had thriving industries, whereas Spain itself had hardly any to speak of. Fernández's patriotism was devoted to a country that desperately needed people. His old-fashioned interlocutors aboard the steamboat struck him as particularly suited to the task, especially once he discovered how numerous and well-connected they were in cities throughout the Balkans and Turkish territories. Fernández was a nationalist—a title that occasionally disguised an abundance of goodwill and generosity which had begun to appear around the turn of the century. In that precise historical moment, Doctor Fernández and his companions believed that, much as Italy had acquired portions of the Ottoman Empire, with the aid of the Sephardim Spain could establish an empire or protectorate of its own in the eastern Mediterranean.

[*Belated proof of Spanish stubbornness*] In the decisive year of 1943, the political milieu determining Spanish foreign policy also included the Duke of Alba—a descendant of Count Egmont, 'the Bloodhound' who had governed the Spanish Netherlands from 1567 to 1573. Deep down, this particular descendant bore the very same stubbornness Friedrich Schiller famously attributed to his family. A perfect storm of German intervention on both informal (Nazi Party) and formal (State) levels fought over the fate of the 1,560 Spanish passport bearers—in vain. The Spanish officials unanimously rejected all arguments and false counter-arguments. They were motivated not by any philan-thropic leanings but by the tattered remains of Spanish national pride, which they administered as if Spain were still in possession of its Armada. In the end, seven women from mixed marriages were identified who had no Spanish passport of their own. These women had been retained at first, but consular protocol stipulated that the German Reich had to let them go as well.

In Persecutions, Practicality Takes Precedence over Mere Morality

Dutch Sephardic philosopher Baruch Spinoza was asked by the treacherous Danish scientist Nicolas Steno, who was researching his work on behalf of the Vatican: Is a man to be held responsible more for the morality of his intentions or for the outcome of his actions? In other words, would it be better if a murder or manslaughter occurred as the result of a series of acts, each of which could individually be considered to have a benign motive—or would it be better if, despite certain malicious intent, no murder or manslaughter actually occurred? Spinoza declined to answer the question directly. What mattered most to him was that no murder or manslaughter took place *under any circumstances*.

However, we humans are mutually responsible for the outcome of all our actions, regardless of the good or evil will of individuals, since mutual actions originate under the influence of various types of willpower and characteristics. Individuals, however, the philosopher continued, are responsible for their intentions according to their own ability to discriminate between good and evil. But good can also mean that which renders the persecution of others harmless, or prevents others' misfortune. So good can also be something that helps one escape evil. Accordingly, Spinoza kept a sailboat (well hidden on the River Scheldt) in which he himself, a protégé or anyone he trusted could make an emergency escape should the political situation take a turn for the worse.

He had, Spinoza added, already seen vast reserves of virtue incapable of preventing politically motivated murder. Conversely, he had also seen countless errors and individually negative intentions which, when taken together, could—almost unintentionally—cause a communal sense of goodness, generosity and unexpected forgiveness, putting a stop to all murders and executions. Thus good is best gathered wherever possible, by the same methods with which we all seek happiness—often on side roads, with no need for God's guidance nor any intentional goodness as its root cause. In this respect, goodness is more of a principle derived from experience than an occasion that can be willed into existence.

The Golem's Ability to Find out the Truth

Rabbi Loew was born Judah Loew ben Bezalel between 1512 and 1525. Only in his later years did he return from exile in Poland to Prague where, now nearly 80, he was elected chief rabbi. At four o'clock one morning (said to have been around 20 Adar 5340, or 17 March 1580), he, his son-in-law and a pupil went to a clay pit along the banks of the Vltava river outside Prague. From the damp clay they formed a figurine with human features. Once it was finished, Rabbi Loew ordered his son-in-law to walk around the Golem seven times and recite a formula, whereupon the clay figure began to glow. Then the pupil who had accompanied Rabbi Loew walked around the figure seven times, whereupon its body started steaming, sprouting hair and fingernails. The Rabbi himself was the last to circle the Golem seven times, repeating a sentence from the creation story: 'And the Lord God formed man of the dust of the ground, and breathed into his nostrils the breath of life; and man became a living soul,' whereupon the Golem's eyes opened.

Another pupil of Rabbi Loew, who had gone to Nurem-berg after the Prague Pogrom, reported that the legend of the Golem was a fiction created to obscure the actual production of this 'protector' (and its subsequent destruction). Indeed, as the people of Israel fled from Egypt towards the Red Sea, wherever they came upon a spring they buried stones or pieces of rock in the ground. These markers would be their salvation if they strayed from the way to the Holy Land, got lost, and had to find their way back. In the meantime, Rabbi Loew's pupil continued, these stones actually moved underground, in the direction of Prague, and had just arrived when Rabbi Loew decided to create the Golem, saviour of the community. Naturally, the clay he used contained said stones. But not even the pupil said a word about just how the figure was created.

The pupil went on to report that the Golem sat in a corner of the Rabbi's room, showing no signs of life. In order to set him into motion, a note bearing the SHEM, the name of God, had to be put under his tongue. Even then the clay figure could not speak, but it was able to recognize the truth. It is said that in 1587 the congregation leader had dropped the Torah scrolls on Yom Kippur, a bad omen. That same night, Rabbi Loew had a dream in which a sequence of letters appeared that he could not decipher, so he instructed the Golem to find an answer to the riddle. Mechanically skimming through the Ten Commandments, the Golem pointed to a verse whose words began with the same letters the rabbi had seen in his dream: 'Thou shalt not covet thy neighbour's wife.' Faced with this verse, the congregation leader broke down in tears and confessed to this selfsame sin. Never again did a Torah scroll fall from the congregation leader's hands.

The Violation of Human Dignity in Ourselves

One member of the conservative milieu at the University of Marburg in 1941 was theologian Tobias Teikner, a church historian, Neo-Kantian philosopher and scientific scholar who was also an esteemed interpreter of Tacitus. He decided to risk meeting with a Jewish scholar who disguised himself behind the Aryan pseudonym Anton Weber from Alsfeld, but was in fact a reincarnation of the MAK'L—namely, the Kabbalist Rabbi Loew. Authentic truth can move through time. This applies to both humans and stones. The Neo-Kantian theologian accepted his opponent of another faith for a nighttime debate. A reminiscence of the Marburg Colloquy, which had almost brought about religious peace centuries before, lingered in the air during their meeting that winter, amid the crisis of 1941.

God chose Israel, the rabbi said, out of free will, not for the prophets' meritoriousness. Therefore, it is incorrect to say that God 'delivered the Jews to the powers of the Third Reich'. 'Israel's humiliation' is indeed a sign, but it is a theologically illegible sign because the free will of God escapes all interpretation. A people has its own natural place. Their separation from this natural place is destructive—not only for those driven into exodus but also for the entire world order. This was precisely what happened when Titus destroyed the temple in Jerusalem in 70 CE. After the people's dispersion, their unity remained in the word. Any destruction of said unity through an act of terror would be tantamount to another 'destruction of the temple'. Each such act desecrates those who wrought the destruction.

The theologian, steward of what remained of the once-powerful Protestant tradition and presumably the reincarnation of the great Philipp Schwartzerdt, was genuinely embarrassed that he could neither form an alliance with the man seated opposite him nor provide many practical answers to the matters they discussed over several hours. He read to the guest a statement by Immanuel Kant, which claimed that every crime against human dignity would destroy the dignity within us all, and therefore such an act would harm not only its the victim but also its perpetrator and all humanity. Although this passage reflected a similar line of reasoning as the rabbi had previously expressed, Teikner seemed to view the written text he had just read as quite different from that of the scholar who had secretly entered his home and spoken of an incipient wave of persecution. To restore a modicum of his own dignity, for his own sake and that of his religious group, he lent his visitor a bicycle for the ride home to Alsfeld, which is how the Gestapo later tracked him down—by following the tyre tracks from the parking lot back to his place (he denied everything). Then, through his network of Protestant colleagues, Teikner managed to get the rabbi to Holland and onto a fishing boat that took him to the British coast. These were all 'expedients of the poor'. The Protestant communities and their guardians no longer had any power over people's souls, be it to protect or persecute. Thus the 'dignity within ourselves' could not be restored at this time (given the modest arsenal of potentially good deeds). It took every last shred of Teikner's faith to deny the true character of this particular period of time. He did not bring this up during their nighttime conversation, either—it struck him as entirely inadequate.

One must pray for salvation, said the rabbi, but not 'too much'. Furthermore, knowledge of the precise time of salvation is forbidden. To even consider it would be to interfere in the will of God. One thing is certain: Immediately before salvation, 'Israel's humiliation will be greater than ever'. Therefore, signs indicating the 'absence of God' can also be interpreted as signs of impending salvation.

As the two men conversed that night, not far from Marburg, the stones of Prague were moving underground; only a small portion of them had been used to make the Golem (after the Golem's destruction they were again buried, and soon followed the other stones on their way northwest).

The building in which Teikner lived was a former trading house, built over seven cellars sealed off from the River Lahn and surrounding groundwater. The two interlocutors, who certainly could have used a topic on which they might agree, could have created a second Golem that night. But they would have had to hide it from the forces of terror. They could not have given their Golem the spark of faith which would have given their creature (born on the second hour of the second day of creation, and therefore in possession of unlimited spiritual potential) power over all perpetrators: THEY GO BLIND, WANDER FALTERINGLY ABOUT, RECOGNIZE NOTHING, AND CAN CATCH NO ONE. But none of that came about. The wandering stones passed right by the attempted religious conversation to which both sides brought so much goodwill.

Fritz Bauer

Dedication

I dedicate these stories to Fritz Bauer, District Attorney of the State of Hesse. I can still picture him standing before me in 1962, the year Adolf Eichmann was executed. The investigations and trials had been chilling. In the evenings, Fritz Bauer often sat in the foyer of the Frankfurter Hof Hotel. Quite alone. Occasionally Alfred Edel, who lived nearby, also quite alone, would visit.

'The moment they come into existence, monstrous crimes have a unique ability,' Bauer once said, 'to ensure their own repetition.' He insisted on the importance of keeping our powers of observation and memory razor sharp. There are 'eerie long-distance effects' and 'non-causal networks' between past and present, between evil attractors and us. They must not be allowed to become more powerful than our own experience.